MW01128348

Dead Wrong

Patricia Dibsie (signature)

PATRICIA DIBSIE

Edited by Margery Craig Farnsworth

outskirts
press

Dead Wrong
All Rights Reserved.
Copyright © 2019 Patricia Dibsie
v2.0

This is a work of fiction. The events and characters described herein are imaginary and are not intended to refer to specific places or living persons. The opinions expressed in this manuscript are solely the opinions of the author and do not represent the opinions or thoughts of the publisher. The author has represented and warranted full ownership and/or legal right to publish all the materials in this book.

This book may not be reproduced, transmitted, or stored in whole or in part by any means, including graphic, electronic, or mechanical without the express written consent of the publisher except in the case of brief quotations embodied in critical articles and reviews.

Outskirts Press, Inc.
http://www.outskirtspress.com

Paperback ISBN: 978-1-9772-0199-7
Hardback ISBN: 978-1-9772-0340-3

Library of Congress Control Number: 2018911254

Cover Photo © 2019 www.gettyimages.com. All rights reserved - used with permission.

Outskirts Press and the "OP" logo are trademarks belonging to Outskirts Press, Inc.

PRINTED IN THE UNITED STATES OF AMERICA

Thanks to Charlee Bear and dozens of other LOVE HEELS Canine Partners who have walked beside us until the end. Truly a mystery how much unconditional love and loyalty you have shown us.

Fifty percent of book sales will be donated to fund and foster more service canines.

Chapter 1

*O*n the last Friday morning of his life, Harry Finnerty's eyes were wide open when the shrieking blast from his alarm clock gave voice to his panic. An empty fear that had no name rumbled in his gut and exploded from his throat in a vinegary belch that made him gag. Something was wrong, very wrong.

Harry dreaded Fridays with the same intense loathing that most people reserved for Monday mornings. He couldn't remember a time when it hadn't been this way. Weekends were always the enemy, a time when loneliness loomed scarier than giant monsters dreamed up by small children at bedtime.

He never learned to make friends as a youngster, instead fine-tuning the art of eavesdropping, then cashing in on secrets. As a teenager, he worked his way from bullying to bribery. His resentment was breeding ground to hone the art of blackmail as the decades rolled by.

Now, at 62, the old man had convinced himself that it was good not to need or depend on another human.

"You and me, Charlee Bear," Harry told the golden retriever camped out by the bedroom door. "We'll have a fine steak tonight."

Not that the hairy red dog needed to be bribed. It was just that the man didn't know any other way to get someone to stick around. Although Harry would never understand, Charlee would have given his life for his best friend.

The huge puppy had attached himself to the man with no friends a year ago on Thanksgiving weekend. They met on a lonely stretch of beach when the abandoned puppy had nowhere to go and the old man was going nowhere. The pooch's mouth was wrapped around an empty bag of liver crackers; "Charlee Bear," read the big red and blue logo.

And that's how Charlee got his name and how Harry found his first and only real friend. Maybe Harry wouldn't have been so distant if he had known that they would only have a short time together. But he didn't know and so he kept the dog at bay.

But Charlee was persistent. By Christmastime, Harry found himself in a pet store shopping for a bed and bowl. He brought them home and placed the cedar bed just outside his door and his heart.

The puppy's boldness grew as fast as his body. The warm bond developing felt odd at first but soon Harry found himself shopping in the meat department for two. He fried up steak and potatoes while confiding secrets to Charlee.

"They think they're so tough, so smart, but I could always put them in their place," Harry had once boasted to Charlee. "I knew them when they were young hoodlums, now they think they're so respectable. Think they're better than me."

Harry knew a lot about the comings and goings of the city's so-called "movers and shakers." His "off-the-record" tape recordings and snapshots had been supplementing his income for years. It wasn't his fault that his only talent couldn't begin to pay for the fine lifestyle to which he felt entitled. His meager paycheck couldn't even cover his growing booze bill.

Harry had come to the West Coast to look for a new beginning, more at his editor's suggestion than a need to flee the cold East Coast winters. He was in his 40s and had a scrapbook of story clippings that made him look like a good fit for a small city newspaper looking to expand. His editor promised a good letter of recommendation; but only if he cleared out within 30 days. Harry moved on before the clock ran out.

Harry found the perfect fit in a trade magazine job column. Happy to get a seasoned writer from a large-city newspaper, *The Vista Journal* editor offered Harry a job as a city columnist. The relationship worked out until he started missing deadlines. Harry eventually found himself demoted to the obituary desk, pounding out the final details of life's winners and losers.

It wasn't long before Harry figured out how to pan gold from pain; he offered to delete troublesome details from obituaries for monetary compensation. Proud survivors wrote checks to manipulate the headlines.

He came up with another angle. Advanced obituaries are written before a famous person's death, so why not Santa Vista's movers and shakers? Why not, indeed.

And that's how Harry came to reconnect with Price Logan of Price Industries—a face from his past and his future benefactor.

On this Friday, nothing out of the ordinary happened to warn him of impending disaster. He went over the day's agenda and dressed in the usual white cotton shirt, black bow tie, and khaki pants. His one "up yours" to the world was different-colored socks; he picked out one green and one red and slipped his feet into brown and white Oxfords.

Harry chugged the last of his black coffee; Charlee woofed down the last breakfast morsels. Harry tucked his thin leather briefcase under his left arm and grabbed the dog bed before heading out the door by eight o'clock sharp.

Like always, Harry tossed the dog bed in the shade of a lemon tree, patted the retriever on the head, and latched the back gate behind him. Neither knew it, but that was to be their last goodbye.

Charlee settled in for a morning nap. Afternoons he went for a stroll with the neighbor across the lawn, then settled his tired bones in his favorite pillow.

The office was a ten-minute stroll, the sole reason Harry had packed up and abandoned the house he first rented when he came West.

Change never came easy; it was always forced on Harry. But a couple of bouts with the law over drinking and driving had forced him to park his old Volvo. He couldn't count on old buddies to bail him out of trouble; he didn't have any friends. He couldn't count on blind luck. If it weren't for bad luck, the old man would have no luck at all.

Chapter 2

*W*hen he arrived at the office, Harry saw a note from his editor slapped on the computer screen: "SEE ME ASAP." Any interruption in his routine made Harry grumpy. He walked into the editor's office and plopped into a chair.

"Close the door," the editor admonished, not looking up from the local section of *The Journal.*

"Uh-huh," Harry sighed, his mind running over the planned daily routine. *First write the lead obit by noon, lunch at the Press Room Bar, and back by three to make my weekly telephone requests for funds. Not a lot, no need for greed.*

Hugh Black had been talking for more than a minute and had expected an outcry from the curmudgeon sitting on the opposite side of his desk. Then he realized Harry wasn't listening, hadn't heard a word. The editor felt dismissed. He continued in a loud voice and bumped the desk to get the old man's attention.

"Harry, it's time to move you over to the copy desk. Our circulation is spiraling downward and we've got to listen to our critics if we want to survive. In that vein, churning out obits isn't working. We're going to bring in a younger writer who can handle the obits but also crank out some features for the younger crowd."

The words "copy desk"—considered the boneyard of every newspaper—went off like a cherry bomb in a young boy's hand, leaving Harry's world shattered and his heart bleeding.

He started to argue but realized the 40-something-year-old boss sitting in judgment could do anything he damn well pleased. Harry didn't have any hold on the man, nothing vile or unsorted to make him see things Harry's way.

His mind played with various scenarios. He could beg, but pride nixed that idea. Threaten? What, to quit? They'd like that.

Defeated, Harry pushed himself out of the chair and closed the door behind him. He didn't hear Hugh: "Sorry, Harry, you've worked long and hard and certainly have my respect, but I'm in a corner here. You understand, right?"

Nope, as usual Harry didn't hear a word when it didn't suit his purpose. He walked to his desk and found several empty cartons piled near his chair. Harry wouldn't give in without a fight. He needed to think; he needed a drink. Or maybe lots of drinks so he wouldn't have to think.

He fled the building and crossed the busy street, paying no attention to the blaring metal monsters that screeched at him to get out of the way. It was early but the neon sign in the Press Room flashed its "open" smile. Harry pushed on the door and headed for his favorite stool at the end of the bar. Murphy poured a shot of Grey Goose on ice and served it up before Harry had time to loosen his tie. He couldn't remember ever seeing Harry here before noon, when he was on an early deadline. People laughed and swore you could set your watch by the old man's comings and goings — in at noon; back to the office by three o'clock sharp. That and the fact that he never left a tip.

He was well into his third shot of courage before he grumped at Murphy, spewing venomous words faster than the rattling tail of an angry sidewinder. The bartender had seen him this mad before but never so defeated. He looked like he'd lost his last friend; but Murphy knew he didn't have a friend to lose. Harry had never let anyone come close.

Mostly he talked about the old days when a reporter could do pretty much as he pleased. Now, the newly popular term "political correctness" was demanded, which only served as a dam on the raging river of emotions churning inside. Harry manipulated his emotions into a controlled flow, and that was about as politically correct as the old man would ever be.

He knew colleagues saw him as a boastful bore, a benign fellow. Harry had made peace with the fact that his colleagues laughed at him behind his back. What they didn't know couldn't hurt him. He felt as sorry for them as he knew they felt for him.

These kids, he called them, they were too young to know the power the press wielded when he was their age. Hell, many were still peeing in their pants and learning to walk. He'd seen new hires come and go; now these kids born of the great world war, the one he had avoided with bad feet. He called them Generation PC; their carefully worded yarns embraced life within the barred confines of a Politically Correct world. Pathetic Clods, that's what they were, he told himself. Enough about them, he had his own problem to solve.

Harry considered his options and settled on a desperate compromise. He chugged the last drops of his fifth and final vodka. He pulled a bill from his wallet, slapped it on the bar, and yelled for Murphy to keep the change.

Murphy picked up the bill and whistled when he eyed Franklin not Jackson staring back at him. "Hell has frozen over, were the only words out of Murphy's mouth as he pocketed the $100 bill. He watched Harry trod back to the newspaper office and found himself saying a silent prayer for the old man.

Harry headed straight for his desk, pushing aside a pile of boxes barricading his chair. He didn't recognize the contents but had more important things on his mind. He took the black address book from his briefcase and settled down for some serious financial negotiating. "No more Mr. Nice Guy," he mumbled to no one in particular.

Chapter 3

*H*arry grabbed a little black book from his briefcase; his eyes scanned the alphabet tabs. His fingers worked their way through his scribbles while his mind calculated names and bank accounts. He stopped on the name Logan. Price Logan.

Harry was interrupted again by an unwanted hand tapping his shoulder. "You're Harry, I'm Lauren Foster, and that's my desk. Let me help you move your personal items over there." Curt, to the point, but still polite, she congratulated herself.

The old man erupted, spewing vile words that, when strung together, were physically impossible. If he expected her to blush, she thought, he was in for a surprise. She was, after all, 26 and had spent a year interning in a New York City newsroom.

Harry turned to give the intruder a piece of his mind but stopped cold when his eyes took in the beautiful young woman who was issuing orders. He wished her away, belched and bellowed when she seemed not to read his mind.

"Scram, vamoose, can't you see I'm working!" His words were slurred but his stare was on the mark. Lauren shivered but stood her ground.

Harry was annoyed with the stranger. He had told her to go away and even turned his back and flicked his shoulder with his fingers as if shooing away a fly. But she kept on talking, insisting that he move both his body and his belongings elsewhere.

Lauren Foster was equally annoyed, her nerves jangled from too much caffeine and not enough life experience to know how to get her way with the older man. Her mind told her to stand her ground; her heart wanted to give him all the time he needed to keep his pride intact while forfeiting his territory. Not an easy task. The more stubborn Harry became, the more determined Lauren behaved.

The old man turned his back again, picked up the telephone, and dialed a string of numbers. The busy signal caused his anger to rise; a cheap gadget was standing between him and his desire to inflict pain on Mr. Price Logan. "Not good enough," he murmured. He cursed the phone, his life, and the broad who wouldn't shut up.

Harry grabbed his coat and headed for the door. This time, he was going to see Mr. Price Logan without an appointment, and no secretary dared to stand between him and his target. Any trouble and Harry figured he'd redo the math and double his demand.

Lauren managed a quick two-step and removed her body from the human tornado's path. She winced as a rush of memory clobbered her senses, taking her back to her grandfather's library. It seemed like yesterday and a lifetime ago all rolled into one cold November afternoon.

Papa Chase had been angry, his face as purple as the man screaming nonsense at her now. Her dear Papa had stormed out to his car and sped off. Nobody told her the who, what, and whys of that afternoon, not even at the funeral a week later. She was only nine years old and was left to deal with the death of her beloved Papa.

Something about Harry and his anger pulled her into the past, and she wanted whatever was going to happen not to happen. Words couldn't make sense of what was in her heart. She just knew that she had to follow Harry out of the building and make sure he got to where he was going...alive.

Harry hailed a cab, and she hailed the one behind, laughing as she heard herself say, "Follow that cab." She had only been in town for a couple of days but recognized the streets. They were headed downtown. The first cab stopped at a ten-story bank building. Her cab stopped a couple of hundred yards south, and she followed the man into the lobby and watched Harry stumble into the express elevator. She checked the lobby directory and noted that the entire tenth floor belonged to one occupant, Price Logan Enterprises.

She pushed the call button and waited. She didn't notice the two men behind her until she had stepped into the elevator, but they took notice of her. Most men did, and it was never subtle. Lauren blushed and steadied herself for the ride to the top. When the doors opened, she saw that Harry was standing near an impressive set of mahogany doors, yelling at a secretary who was more determined to get her way than to give in to this tiresome man.

Lauren blocked their way and issued a mandate: "Get a cab and I'll get him home." Harry spewed threats to the men all the way to the lobby. "The big man will pay for this. Tell him maybe it's not about money anymore. Tell him if he thinks I'm going to go away, he's dead wrong. YOU tell him Harry Finnerty said so."

The two men stepped from behind Lauren and charged at Harry, each picking up an arm. They read the secretary's body language. Harry was on his way down the elevator and back on the street.

They poured Harry into the cab, and Lauren told the cabdriver to take them back to the newspaper office. When they arrived, Lauren scanned the sidewalk for a familiar face to help her get him home. But nothing went as planned. Harry bolted from the cab and made a beeline to the Press Room. Lauren followed him in and pulled out the barstool next to Harry. Two hours later, Lauren convinced Harry to go home, a short walk with her, and then she promised to leave him alone.

They were almost home when it happened. A car raced down the middle of the street toward them. The black sedan swerved at the last second and took aim. That's what Lauren remembered. Harry pushed her away from him, and a moment later she heard the thud. Harry's crumpled body lay still, his breathing shallow. Her arm hurt, her blouse was torn where her shoulder collided with the road, but she crawled over to Harry and heard him whisper, "Charlee Bear."

Lauren had not seen the dog coming but there he was. The huge, red retriever bounded from between parked cars and headed straight for Harry. His brown eyes searched Harry's face. The canine lay down next to his friend, his head resting on Harry's chest till the last breath exited his master's body.

The moaning sounds from the dog were both eerie and comforting to Lauren. When the ambulance pulled up, she collared the dog with her dress belt and the two sat on a nearby curb.

Lauren didn't know anything about dogs, never had a pet growing up, but she took comfort in stroking the fur behind the dog's ears.

She'd had the hell scared out of her and didn't feel steady on her feet. She needed some time to just sit and think. What the hell had just happened?

The one thing she was sure of: This was no accident.

Chapter 4

*L*auren waited for the police to finish with the ambulance crew before turning their attention to the only witness. She was still shaking, partly from the chill in the air but more so from the chill that ran down her spine.

If Harry hadn't pushed her out of the way, she would be lying on the ground next to him. She knew she didn't know anyone who hated her enough to kill her. She couldn't say the same about the man who lay lifeless under the white sheet.

She hadn't felt intimidated by Harry; his anger was more like a mask some people put on to keep the world at bay. His anger seemed more lonely than malevolent. But, she had to admit to herself, she knew next to nothing about Harry Finnerty.

Mentally, she put the last half hour on rerun and played back the incident over and over. Every time, she came to the same conclusion. That car had aimed for Harry, came faster as it came closer. The black sedan was like every other car on the road, nothing special to help the police identify it. Shattered glass from a headlight was scattered around Harry's body. She had a couple of wounds where glass grazed her arm and drew blood. And her head hurt from the fall.

"No, no need to go to the hospital, it's just scratches," she told the officer. When she rubbed her temple, the red dog leaned in and put his head on her shoulder. She put an arm around the hound and found herself trying to comfort the animal. He whimpered and suddenly she felt very protective.

The police asked her if the dog was hers and she had to admit that, no, it belonged to the dead man. The younger officer volunteered to call county animal control for a wagon to pick up the newly homeless dog. She found herself choking as the lie she concocted formed words and poured from her mouth. "Harry's wife will want Charlee home when she hears the news. Let me take him."

The officer checked his notes and looked suspiciously at Lauren. "Says here he's not married, lives in a cottage down the street on Grand. Lives alone. Besides, most of us have picked up Harry for being drunk and deposited him home. Most likely, Harry walked in front of the car and the driver was too scared to stop."

She tightened her grip on Charlee and told the policeman she would take responsibility for the dog. Her mind was figuring out just how she was supposed to sneak a 60-plus-pound golden into her "no pets" hotel room. Mere detail. Nobody was going to take this dog to the pound.

She had a plan, the usual plan when things went mind-numbingly haywire. Call Marissa. The two had depended on one another for solutions to life's big and little problems since freshman year in college. They were dorm roomies and took to one another immediately. They shared classes, dreams, shoes, and clothes. Same height, same size, same shoulder-length blonde hair; their birthdays were separated by less than 24 hours. And the two had shared Marissa's parents since their sophomore year in college.

Lauren had lost her parents in an automobile accident at age 13 and had gone to live with her mother's sister, Sarah Chase. Sweet Aunt Sarah had brought Lauren up to believe in God, the Good Book, and herself. "Dream it and then make it happen," she heard her aunt say over and over. "Talk it over with God, then put your dream into action," read the sign over her bed. Growing up was filled with the usual turmoil, but the steady hand of her aunt steered her clear of big trouble. Her teen years were uneventful, and she felt blessed.

Aunt Sarah was so proud when a dozen colleges accepted Lauren's application for admittance. In the end, she chose a small school in Illinois to be near her aunt. Not a year had passed before her aunt's heart ran out of time.

Marissa stepped in to help her make the dozens of decisions associated with the death of a loved one. Her parents, Ben and Joan Taylor, insisted Lauren come home to stay with them the summer between freshman and sophomore years. By the next Christmas, her holiday presents were signed "from Mom and Dad." It was a blessing she never took for granted. She had parents to love her and, best of all, a sister for the first time in her life.

Lauren's mind processed the obvious. Find a telephone and call Marissa. *She'll know what to do.* Lauren looked at the address on Charlee's collar and headed for 2121 Grand Court, No. 3. Harry's door was closed but not locked. She opened the door and used the telephone to call Marissa.

Marissa's answering machine picked up the call. Lauren left Harry's number, said it was important, leaving out the details. Her second call was to the City Desk at *The Journal.* Her call was transferred to the city editor where she repeated the story of Harry's death, assured him she wasn't injured but, yeah, just a little shaken. He added that he'd have another staffer cover the accident and for her to get some rest.

A knock at the door interrupted the phone conversation. Betty Woods introduced herself as the neighbor next door and looked relieved when she saw Charlee.

"I was supposed to be watching him, but for no reason he just cleared the fence and ran off," she told Lauren. "I watch Charlee in the day while Harry's at work, least he stays on the gated patio we share. I make sure he has water, and nobody steals him. Harry was a loner; never liked anyone except for his dog. They kind of adopted each other last year."

Another knock at the door, this time the police with the manager. They wanted to speak to all the tenants, wanted to find out if Harry had been arguing with anybody lately. Betty looked bewildered. Lauren voice was soft and steady. "Harry's dead. He was hit a couple of blocks from here."

Betty managed an unaffected "Oh," but her eyes filled with tears. The two had been neighbors for several years. Betty hoped that someday it would turn into something more. It wasn't so much that she took a shine to Harry as much as the unacceptable thought of dying an old maid. Her tears were for the death of her dreams, not so much for Harry.

"Are you keeping Charlee? I have his bed if you are," Betty told Lauren. "He likes his bed, makes him feel like he has a permanent home. You know Harry found him abandoned on the beach."

An idea struck Lauren and she asked Betty if she would watch Charlee while she searched for a place that allowed pets. The manager chimed in that Harry's place was available and that he could make her a good deal if she signed an "as is" lease. If not this cottage, No. 6 would be available at the end of next week, "hundred dollars more a month," the manager added.

Lauren jumped at the chance to pick up Harry's lease. The one-bedroom cottage faced the ocean, and the roar of the surf calmed her. Problem solved.

The bigger question Lauren faced was the "murder" of Harry; she was convinced it was no mere hit-and-run accident, even though that's how the police read it.

Lauren wished everyone would leave her cottage. She liked the sound of "her" cottage. Her body was crashing from the downward spiral of adrenaline that had kept her on her feet and moving. Suddenly she was tired, very tired.

The police said the report most likely would be filed as a hit-and-run. Betty left for her evening shift at the nearby diner, and the landlord said tomorrow would be soon enough to make Lauren's tenancy official.

Lauren didn't even bother to go back to the hotel for her toothbrush and pajamas. She found a tube of Crest and put some on her finger, then gave her teeth a once-over. She curled up on Harry's unmade bed and Charlee took his rightful place at the door.

A short time later, she woke with a start to the sound of a jangling telephone in the next room. She opened her eyes, looked around, but couldn't remember where she was.

Lauren stumbled to the doorway and stepped over the fluffy red dog. She picked up the receiver a dozen rings later.

Marissa felt relief when she heard her sister's voice. There was trouble in the voice she heard on her message machine. If Lauren wasn't injured, Marissa figured the two of them could solve any problem.

"I think I witnessed a murder," Lauren stuttered. "The police put it down as an accident, but it wasn't. I know it was murder."

Marissa demanded the who, what, when, and why of it all. Lauren could give her the answers to all but the last. She didn't know why, hadn't a clue, but Lauren was determined to ask enough questions to satisfy her curiosity. Marissa had known her sister long enough to be sure of that.

"Let me think about this and we'll talk about it tomorrow when we're in Seattle," Marissa said. "You sound tired and we both know you don't make the best decisions when you're in a blur."

The same moment her mind tripped on the word "Seattle," mental clouds faded, and Lauren remembered her parents' 30th anniversary bash. "I forgot in all the chaos, I have a noon flight." Lauren laughed. "Meet you at the car rental desk." She hung up the phone and headed to the bedroom, tripping over Charlee. She threw on some shorts and a shirt, slipped into sandals, and headed out.

This time she paused at the doorway, stared down at Charlee, and told him to stay. She reached down, patted him on the head, and told him she was going to the hotel to check out and promised to be right back. Later, she promised herself, she would figure out how to communicate with a dog. They were family now.

Chapter 5

*P*rice paced in front of his desk, his eyes playing a game of Ping Pong, bouncing from the huge gold watch wrapped around his wrist and back again to the telephone on his desk. One glowed, ticking off the seconds heading for seven o'clock. The other, the light to his private line, was as dark as his foreboding mood.

He strode across the room, threw open mahogany doors that hid his stash of Johnnie Walker Black. He was about to violate his cardinal rule: No alcohol until work was done for the day. No alcohol after eleven either; it interfered with a good night's sleep. Price sneered when he realized seven and eleven were the perfect words to describe his predicament. His life, or any promise of one outside of prison, came down to a throw of the dice.

When the phone finally disrupted his walk on the dark side, Price hesitated to pick it up. The big man found himself more frightened than curious. Had the job been done? Was he right to give Virgil so much responsibility?

He picked up the receiver, said hello, and heard the voice on the other end confirm, "I did what you said, used a stolen black sedan to kill Harry." The unnamed voice continued the monologue, relaying that he pulled the car into the belly of a moving van parked in an alley several blocks away. Virgil said he checked for anyone who might be looking at what he was doing. Didn't see anyone, so he slammed the big metal door closed and jumped into the driver's seat. He put the truck into drive and headed east to the freeway for the six-hour trek to the Mexican border.

"Drove it down to Mexico, just like you told me, boss," Virgil continued. "Stopped to call you at the bar like you told me. So, what now, Mr. Logan?"

Virgil was mentally counting hundred-dollar bills, so many, his math skills were stretched to the limit. One thing he knew, there were lots of hundreds in five thousand bucks.

The grin on his face was wiped clean by hail of bullets targeting the row of pay phones lining the back wall. Virgil and three other men fell to the ground and drowned in red pools of death.

A second before he died, Virgil knew he had been wrong about hitting the jackpot. Dead wrong.

On the other end of the phone, a smile of satisfaction rushed across Price's lips. His scheme had been successful. He was rid of Harry; he was rid of Virgil. And nobody knew he was the anonymous caller who tattled to the gangs on the street about a van loaded with drugs crossing the border. Word had it, the truck would be at Tio's bar right after sunset.

He tipped his glass, took a swig, and congratulated himself out loud. "To the bad people who do bad things." Then he hung up the phone and finished his thought. "And to the stupid people who do stupid things and pay a huge price."

He laughed, then gulped the rest of his whiskey. Point. Set. Game.

If Price had stayed on the line a moment longer, he would have heard the dead giveaway of a phone tap. But he was too full of himself and too in need of another glass of scotch.

Chapter 6

It was late, the office should have closed hours ago, but last-minute deadlines kept the staff at their desks past sundown. San Francisco FBI Chief Gus Hagey buzzed his secretary, instructed her to collect Special Agent Bill Stevens and bring him to his office. And he added, "Do it now but don't appear anxious; just tell him the price for the new project is too high."

The secretary had been around long enough to know this was a code phrase which translated into trouble; whether it was Bill's trouble or Gus's trouble she couldn't hazard a guess. She wasn't paid to guess; none of them was. Just the facts.

When Bill walked in, he knew what the problem was but needed details. Banking and development entrepreneur Price Logan was the essence of trouble. The FBI had been after him for quite a while, and frustration was the only thing they had to show for three long years of toil.

A new hot-shot agent had put a bug in Price's telephone. Didn't ask, didn't tell, until this morning when it looked like the bank executive had put out a hit in Mexico. Word on the street was drugs were involved. The agent heard bits and pieces of the phone call, ending with a spray of bullets. Price got the last words, said something about "bad people do bad things" or something like that. Then silence. The agent came straight to the top man, expecting kudos for providing the bait that would finally land the Bureau one big fish.

The inexperienced agent waltzed in with a grin as wide as sunset just before the ocean swallows the sun whole. He left with his walking papers; the mess now belonged to Gus. If his boss caught wind of this, Gus would pay the price—a boot in the seat of his pants that would land the Bureau chief somewhere in Montana. If he was lucky. This close to retirement could spell the end of a promised promotion and raise in benefits before he turned in his papers and retreated to his lake house in Colorado. He just needed to keep his head down and his plate clean for 62 days.

Gus was good at problem solving. He jotted each point on a piece of yellow legal paper in order of importance. He drew a thick line at the bottom of the page and, like always, came away with a solution. Like math, it was a science to him. Two wrongs never added up to a right, and the law was his abacus.

New agents could learn a lot from him, and they signed a waiting list to work with the old man before he called it quits. Most were eager to please him, and some, like the last jackass, were too eager.

Gus shrugged his shoulders and circled the solution he thought could best serve his needs and the needs of the Bureau. It would give him time to get the bug out of the phone and go on as if nothing had gone off the track. The solution, a patchwork of promises sealed with a promotion boiled down to two words: Tower Stadler.

But Gus couldn't approach the man; orders this high up could be taken all wrong. He needed to back up the investigation before the illegal tap became public, then get a fresh pair of eyes on the situation. Money laundering was serious business, but if what the fired agent had told him was true, the investigation could lead to charges of drug trafficking and murder. Gus had come to loathe the likes of Price Logan and the crooked game he played, seeming to always come out the winner.

Gus considered it an obligation to put this man behind bars before he turned in his papers. Time was getting short; he had just two months to make good on the promise he had made to himself.

Bill Stevens was familiar with the Price Logan debacle. So many times they thought they had him, only to learn the agents had been fooled and were looking in the wrong neighborhood. The man was smart, sneaky smart, and always a step ahead. Okay, several steps ahead.

"Gus, how bad is it this time?" he asked. The chief shook his head and handed the paper to Bill. Stevens let out a long whistle.

"No judge signed off on this," Hagey added, not even looking up. "He just got it into his head to fast-track our investigation. If he put the bug in the phone like he says and didn't broadcast it, then we have a chance to keep it in this office.

"The way I have it figured, this Stadler agent can pick up the investigation with nothing said about what we've learned today," Hagey said. "All we've lost is a little time. Get Stadler to Santa Vista, and don't give him any more details than necessary. Good man, too bad he knows it. Always cripples a guy in the long run to be too sure of himself."

"Yeah, but you've got to admit this guy is good. All the senior agents team up with him and get results," Stevens said. "I got the credit, but it was Tower who put all the pieces together in that Los Angeles robbery investigation. His plan, my lead, and I got all the credit. Press ate it up. Still can picture Tower storming off. Don't think he cares for me a twit. This letter coming from me will likely be a slap in the face. Your call."

"Do it today," the big man said, ripping the paper in shreds as if magically making the problem disappear.

Stadler was at home in Seattle when the new orders were delivered less than an hour after the two men had devised a plan.

Chapter 7

*T*ower Stadler wasn't smiling; the grin that had danced on his lips when he eagerly ripped open the envelope only seconds ago erupted into a tsunami of emotion. The flames in his belly surged and stuck in his throat. The beer he chugged to cool the ache inside only served to fan the fire. He could feel the heat rise to his forehead, confirmed by a bead of sweat that splattered on the opened letter.

The 35-year-old FBI agent read the letter a second time. His rambunctious spirit plotted revenge while waves of reality splashed cold water on his resolve. Truth was, Tower had expected his next assignment to bring both adventure and recognition. He was due. "Past due," he muttered out loud. The ten-year veteran knew he was ready; he was good. Begrudgingly, coworkers noticed his knack at targeting cases and zeroing in on the culprit. He basked in the nickname "one percenter," and he had not made many friends by being right so much of the time.

Early in his career, Tower was singled out to work with a team of heavy hitters. Success came often, and the headlines sang the praises of his mentors but never a mention of the prominent role he had played. He had made no secret of his dissatisfaction, and his moods were beginning to border on mutiny.

Well, fate had handed him the envelope with his future signed and sealed. And it delivered a final blow. Translated, it read: "Go to hell."

His personal "hell" was a small town in Central California. The letter spelled out his future. He was to report to the agent he liked the least, the one man who had taken all the credit for a case Tower figured was his ticket to promotion.

With only a three-day heads-up, he was ordered to report to Agent William Stevens in San Francisco. From there, his assignment was in a town south of the sprawling city. South of the big time. South was where his career was heading.

He dropped his head into his hands and decided to head to the neighborhood tavern one last Friday night.

He was glad his father hadn't lived to see his prophecy fulfilled. Tom Stadler told him not to dream; not to try to be better than what life had meant for you. Tower never bought into his father's pessimism. The son didn't know the details of how badly life had disappointed the father. His father never talked much about his childhood, or the war or much of anything else.

He knew his dad had left home the day after Pearl Harbor was bombed and joined the army. He must have seen a lot of death and suffering; that's how the son explained his father's utter retreat from life. He met Julianna in France and brought her to America in the summer of 1945. The couple settled in Washington State and stayed pretty much to themselves. His mother was content with a peace she had never known. It wasn't in her nature to talk about the past, so the mother and father had respected their mutual dislike for all things yesterday.

But not the son, who grew into a physical mirror-image of his father. Tower woke up every morning ready to explore the world, eager to carve out his share and stake a claim. He craved excitement. He lived for challenges and that was something his father neither understood nor acknowledged. They lived under the same roof, but their thoughts were worlds apart.

Tower combed through his father's meager belongings after he died but got no answers to myriad questions rummaging through his brain. His father was, and would always remain, an enigma. His mother died a year later, and Tower understood that loneliness was the cause. Her life began when she met Tom Stadler, and her spirit died the day Tom's eyes closed for the last time. She didn't say much in the year it took for her body to follow her spirit.

Tower buried them side-by-side with one gravestone that bore the inscription "Tom and Julianna Stadler. Together in life; not separated in death." He didn't bother with dates. No one would mourn the loss of Tom and Julianna except their only son, Tower.

The only question his mom answered was how he got his name. Julianna met Tom in Paris, in the late afternoon when the famous landmark cast a shadow on the landscape. It was the only part of history carried from past to present.

Chapter 8

*L*auren poured some dry food into a bowl and placed it in front of Charlee. "Don't expect breakfast in bed every morning," she told the dog. It felt good having someone around to talk to, better than just talking to herself, even if Charlee didn't understand a word she was saying.

But the way those huge brown eyes stared at her, combined with the tilt of his massive head, made her wonder if she was wrong. Maybe he did understand every word she was saying. *Note to self: Get a basic book all about dogs—the big, independent kind.*

The cab was waiting when Lauren slammed the front door on her way out. Lauren's next-door neighbor Betty peeked her head around the kitchen curtain and waved.

"Charlee is having breakfast, and I'll be back in an hour," Lauren yelled while racing for the taxi. She tossed the keys on Betty's doormat, in case Charlee's normal schedule dictated a walk. She didn't know the dog's routine but counted on Betty to help her figure it all out. And she reminded herself to ask Betty to watch Charlee while she was away in Seattle.

Taking responsibility for someone other than herself made Lauren feel like an adult. Probably a good idea to start with a dog and work her way up. The thought made her giggle.

The ride was less than ten minutes to the hotel, and she figured a half hour to pack and the same ten-minute ride back to her new digs. She planned to leave the cottage untouched until she returned from Seattle. Then, she would have to tackle some serious sorting and sanitizing. It had to be done but better later than sooner.

Once in the hotel room, she tossed her toiletries into a tote and grabbed clothes off their hangers, folding and placing them into a large suitcase. She filled a denim carry-all with photo frames, the few books she cherished, and her alarm clock. Lauren called the desk to get someone to help bring her meager belongings downstairs and put them in a taxi.

She felt a momentary sadness. At 26, her life's possessions could fit in the trunk of a taxi. She had stored Aunt Sarah's collection of furniture, books, and paintings. They were dear to her, but she hadn't really dealt with the loss. Having so many memories surrounding her felt suffocating. She did what came easiest: bury feelings and plow forward.

She shook her head, willing to leave the past so she could put her full attention on the present. She had a mental list of things she had to do before catching her flight.

When she arrived back at the cottage, Lauren found Charlee asleep on the patio, his head shaded by a mature lemon tree. He opened an eye when he heard the gate latch squeak. A second later his tail was in motion, ears perked up, and he was on his feet to give Lauren a proper greeting. Just before impact, the canine put on his padded brakes, coupled with the most wonderful noises. Some day she would understand all this commotion, just not this day. She petted his head and told Charlee she missed him too. She thought if he could understand her, that would be exactly what he wanted to hear.

A laugh came from Betty as she approached with an armload of groceries. "Never did that to me, never got a greeting like that. I was going to ask you if I could adopt him, but it's pretty clear he's picked you," she said.

"I'm going to need some help, never had a dog growing up in the city," Lauren confessed. "I need to go up to Seattle for a few days. Can you take him while I'm gone? I can pay you."

"Sure can, Charlee is easy," Betty said. "I'll feed him and take him for walks. He's a good boy, seeing how young he is, never chews anything but his toys. I'll just toss his bed under that tree during the day, and between visits to neighborhood kids, he'll find his way home for naps. Charlee has his own fan club."

She told Lauren she was used to feeding Charlee dinner when Harry stayed too long at the bar. And she added a piece of advice. "Harry never locked the door, but I think you should. I'll make me another key while you're gone."

As for money changing hands, she told Lauren that taking pay for keeping Charlee would be stealing. "Thanks for the offer, but no thanks."

The two women shook hands and Charlee put his paw on Lauren's wrist to seal the deal. Whatever was going on, he wanted in on it too. The humans laughed, and the dog barked his approval. It felt good to laugh again.

Charlee was napping when Lauren left for the airport, or at least his eyes were shut. But his tail thumped, code for "have fun, see you in a few days." Or if dogs could talk, that's what Lauren would have wanted to hear him say.

Lauren was glad she noticed the big yellow book on the kitchen counter. *The 100 Greatest Dog Training Tips of All*, with a subtitle promising "the only dog tips you'll EVER need." She grabbed the tome, stuffed it in her tote to read on the plane from San Francisco to Seattle. First, though, she had to endure a one-hour bus ride to the city. She opened the taxi door and told the driver to take her to the bus station.

Across the street from the cottage, the driver of a blue sedan took note of her leave and followed her for the second time that day. He had been parked there, observing her every move from the moment she walked the big red dog home yesterday. He followed her to the hotel earlier, and tailed her, unnoticed, back again. He spied her stopping to talk to the neighbor and crept close enough to listen. He reported the conversation to the man who hired him and was told to call back when he was sure she left town.

He telephoned the boss after he witnessed the bus pull out with Lauren and her luggage on board. The man on the other end of the line thanked him and told him he wasn't needed further. He could pick up his check at the detective agency Monday morning.

The owner of the detective agency called his client and confirmed that the person of interest wouldn't be back until Monday. He reported other details his detective had collected during the past 18 hours.

He was thanked and promised a substantial check for the good work.

Case closed.

Chapter 9

A blue and orange moving van pulled up to the Ocean View Cottages on Grand Avenue moments after the rubber tires disappeared into the belly of the Seattle-bound jet.

Lauren loved to fly; it was just the takeoff and landing that put the fear of God in her. Two things always happened: She forgot to breathe and she remembered to pray.

The last couple of years, Lauren had neglected Sunday morning services, opting instead to press the snooze button on her alarm. Aunt Sarah would not have approved. Feeding your soul was as important as feeding your stomach, she preached. Then relented, adding, "The other six days count the same; just make sure you talk to God on a regular basis."

Thinking about her aunt brought less pain and more sweet memories as the months and years wore on. Not that she would ever get over the loss; she kept Aunt Sarah close in her heart.

She wondered why airplane rides took her back in time. Her mind jumped back more than a decade to the last day and the last conversation she had with her parents. The memories were on rewind and replay; pain played in the background.

At 12, she just wanted her parents to leave her alone. Her dream was to wake up and be 18, rid of her parents' unreasonable rules and restrictions. Daughter and parents had never been close, and she was painfully aware her arrival into the world was unplanned. They tried to raise her the best way they knew: They hired a nanny. Mother and father were gone more than they were home, which suited Lauren fine.

On her 13th birthday, they surprised her with reservations at a fancy restaurant and insisted that she swap her jeans for a dress. It was just one more thing to confirm how little her parents knew about her. She wanted to go to the mall with her friends and eat pizza. Lauren stormed to her bedroom, slammed the door, and yelled she wished they were dead. Her parents slammed the front door on their way out to dinner.

Lauren fell asleep waiting for them to come home. She wanted to apologize. She never meant the words that came out of her mouth, not really. She would tell them she was sorry; always they forgave her outbursts. Tonight, the three would head for the kitchen to cut a special four-layer chocolate cake. First, there were 13 pink candles to make a wish on and blow out.

But it never happened. Her parents never returned home. She never got to say she was sorry. Her nanny was the one to break the news of their deaths, then try to comfort the angry teenager. Her parents died at the hands of a drunk driver on the way home from dinner.

The next day, Aunt Sarah arrived to take Lauren to live with her in Chicago. Never motherly, she said she hadn't a clue and was too old to learn. But she had loved her dear niece from the moment she held her the day Lauren was born.

Every August, aunt and niece spent the month riding and roping at a dude ranch in Wyoming or sunning and surfing on a California beach. The summer stays started when Lauren was five years old; both parents needed to be in Europe for the month. Lauren looked forward to the last week, saved for a visit with Papa Chase on the lake in Chicago.

These monthly vacations lasted four years, until Papa's unexpected death the fourth week of August after Lauren turned nine. The young girl never saw her aunt cry, but the loss of her father changed her. Aunt Sarah turned inward; she decided to celebrate her father's life with random acts of kindness. Lauren was devastated but followed her aunt's lead and never cried. She wanted to know why God took her precious Papa but no one ever explained.

Lauren's mother, her aunt's sister, didn't fly home for the funeral. Lauren had never really forgiven her for that; neither did Aunt Sarah, and the bond between aunt and niece grew stronger.

Sweet memories. Painful memories.

Lauren was jolted back to the present when the stewardess announced that the plane had reached its flying altitude and passengers were free to unbuckle their seat belts. Her mind danced with equal parts relief and guilt. *Note to self: Say extra prayers tonight.*

She decided to treat herself to white wine and had just pulled her carry-on tote up to her lap when the stewardess came back with a glass of sauvignon blanc. Coordination wasn't one of her strong suits, and it didn't surprise Lauren when she knocked the glass sideways. The wine splashed on the yellow dog book, which fell to the floor.

Lauren sopped up the wine with the dozen paper napkins the stewardess handed her. She didn't blush. It happened too often for Lauren to be either embarrassed or surprised. She just dabbed the liquid and reached down to retrieve her book. A black-and-white photo floated from between the pages and landed at her feet. She rescued it from the floor, wiped it dry, and gave the photo a cursory glance before stashing it in the pocket of her favorite khaki jacket. Two guys, she noticed. Nobody she recognized; not important.

Lauren decided to nap and put the book on the fold-down tray to dry. She was jostled awake by the stewardess tapping her shoulder. Time to put her chair in the upright position and fasten her seat belt. She had slept the entire flight. Lauren looked out the cabin window and saw a sprawling city beckoning the plane to come on down.

Harry's mishap, the cottage, and even Charlee Bear took a backseat to the excitement of spending the weekend with her mom, dad, and sister, Marissa. She was blissfully unaware of the upset unfolding at 2121 Grand Court.

One man checked under the mat for a door key at Cottage #3; the other was antsy to finish loading the donations before it got dark. Betty saw the men and came outside, and Charlee followed. She wanted to know what they were doing. Charlee growled his disapproval. Betty pushed Charlee back into her cottage and closed the door.

"Here to pick up some items," one mumbled. "Supposed to be Tuesday but somebody overbooked so we were hoping to do it today. Do you know where Lauren Foster is? We need her to sign so we can finish before dark."

Betty was late for work and made a snap decision to let the guys go ahead and clear out the stuff on their list. Her instincts were confirmed when she saw that the items were being taken to the local Goodwill store. The one-bedroom cottage was crammed with books and furniture; Betty didn't think twice about the idea of Lauren wanting to make room for some of her own belongings. She let the two men enter, thinking that she had done a good deed for her newest neighbor. They were going to be friends, she told herself, and more than anything, she wanted a friend.

"Lock the door on your way out," she said before heading out. "And put the key under my doormat." Betty hummed a favorite tune as she made the two-block trek to the diner.

The men were gone when Betty got home shortly after midnight. She bent over to retrieve the key from under her mat. Betty groaned. She didn't know what hurt more, her feet or an aching back. She was getting too old for this gig but needed the work for rent and food. She gulped down a couple of aspirins and let Charlee out for a last chance to empty his bladder. She said Harry's magic words, "Get busy," and Charlee squatted; she hoped he would never learn to lift his leg to pee. This was so much easier to clean. She sprayed the yellow pool with a garden hose, and the two headed for the overstuffed sofa to sack out in front of the TV.

Life was looking up. Betty had found someone to be a friend. Her gentle sighs grew into a thundering snore. Charlee slid off the sofa and padded to the bedroom, where he snuggled on top of a fluffy comforter.

If Charlee could talk, he would have told Lauren to come home.

Chapter 10

*I*f he hadn't forgotten his sunglasses. If he hadn't turned the moving truck around to go get them. And if he'd remembered to fill the tank before this last job, Tony wouldn't be sitting on the side of the road waiting for Triple A to bring him a gallon of gas. He was alone; the guy assigned to help him pack left an hour before the job was done to meet up with his girlfriend at a nearby bar.

It was after seven o'clock when he pulled the loaded truck into the driveway only to discover that the city's donation center was padlocked shut. No one was there to give Tony a pass, and he was sure this time he'd lose this job too. He'd been warned not to be late, warned twice and put on probation.

So, when the stranger with the gun walked up and tapped on the van's window, he opened the cab door, raised his hands in defeat, and kiddingly said, "Why don't you just shoot me and put me out of my misery."

The man obliged. No one was close enough to hear the bullet discharge. No one heard Tony's whimpers as his body fell out of the van and folded to the ground in a heap.

The hijacker with the gun tucked the .45 in his jacket pocket, shoved Tony into the nearby shrubs, then slowly drove the van across town to the warehouse district. It was his second truck this month, easy money.

He was so pleased with himself he failed to notice the dark sedan tailing him back to the vacant warehouse district. The man jumped from the truck and was busy trying to fit a key in the lock when he was struck over the head from behind. The thief never felt the blow to his ego or to his head. His eyes would be closed for hours.

The man in the sedan pulled him out on the street, wiped the steering wheel clean, and removed the keys. He hot-wired the car, messy as an amateur car thief. Then Price Logan went back to the truck and got into the driver's seat.

Price owned a warehouse in the same district. The ten-minute drive from where he was to where he wanted to be was void of traffic after dark. The businesses there employed mostly union workers, and when five o'clock came there was a mass exodus. Within fifteen minutes, the road out was empty.

Price drove down a wide ramp to the warehouse garage door, put the truck in park, then looked around before he got out of the cab. Never could tell, someone might want to do unto him as he had just done unto another. His whole body laughed, and he breathed evenly for the first time that night. His original plan was to break into the donation center and hot-wire the truck, but life took a liking to him this night and gave him a free pass. Easy pickings, he thought.

He drove the truck inside the cavernous warehouse, shut off the motor, and went in search of the light switch. He had been here more than once, but always in the day time and always with a crew. He headed for the wall nearest the doorway and flicked on a flashlight. The electrical panel was there, but before he flipped the lights on, he needed privacy. He closed the garage doors, bolted the locks, then switched on the lights.

When he pulled up on the handle to expose the truck's cargo, Price was forced to leap left and back lest he be buried in an avalanche of junk. He had never been in Harry's cottage; he had no clue how the man lived, only how he died. His face turned ugly and his mouth spewed every four-letter word he knew, some twice.

Price knew exactly what he was looking for but had no clue where to find it. He had the weekend to sift through the contents; he had told his secretary he would be out of town until Monday.

Price divided the contents into three piles: Yes. No. Maybe.

At the end of six hours, the "no" pile had grown to six feet. The "yes" and "maybe" piles were smaller, and he looked up and voiced a "thank you" to no one in particular.

The empty warehouse made him uneasy. He felt pulled back to a moment he'd spent a lifetime trying to erase from his memory. Darkness and doom loomed large in this warehouse.

Searching for the blackmailer's film forced him to relive a nightmare that had haunted him just shy of four decades. It started out as foolish fun. He and his buddy, Tom Stadler, guzzled vodka before picking up a coed on campus. The boys headed for a secluded park, determined to lose their virginity.

The misstep that followed spelled disaster. The two teenagers, drunk and careless, forced themselves on the girl and got too rough when she demanded to leave. She ended up with a broken neck;

they ended up with broken lives. And Harry Finnerty ended up with film fodder to barter for friendship and maybe a little cash.

But the senselessness of the night before and its consequences came crashing down on Sunday, December 7, 1941. As word spread of the surprise attack at Pearl Harbor in Hawaii, both young and old made decisions that day that would affect the rest of their lives.

Price made the decision to stay put and finish his degree; Tom joined the army to flee. The two never saw or spoke to one another again. Price didn't want to know if Tom made it home from the war, and he didn't care. That part of his life was dead and buried, literally and figuratively.

The kicker — neither Tom nor Price had a moment's pleasure before each was sentenced to a life of pain and regret. No regret for what had happened on Price's part. He figured the girl got what she asked for and he was there to see that she got it. His only fear was what could happen if the truth ever surfaced.

Price continued to pore through Harry's belongings to find the one thing he figured belonged to him—photos and negatives Harry had held over his bank account for so many years. Price would find and destroy the film so he could get on with his business plans to make millions on a new project.

He decided to take a break and eat the turkey on rye he'd packed, along with a dill pickle and potato chips. He took a big swig from a thermos filled with black coffee and thought how good a cigarette would taste. Price felt if he were ever going to start smoking again, this would be the moment. He was glad he hadn't opened the bottle of whisky; he needed to stay focused and angry. Anger was high-octane fuel and he needed it to make it through the night.

Price hadn't guessed that Harry was prone to hoarding. He had a dozen cameras, and boxes of articles he had written during his newspaper career spanning college to present.

Boxes and boxes of photos, but not one print taken of Tom and Price after a football win against a rival college on that fateful December afternoon. He couldn't find any of the two pals and that stupid girl. Tina, he recalled, Tina Stewart. He remembered combing the local section of the newspaper for weeks, searching for anything about her disappearance. Dumb broad. Tramp. Whore.

He could kill Harry for making all this so difficult. And then he remembered that he already did. The thought didn't make the chore any less arduous. Price was forced to watch Harry's life in photos while sifting through his junk. Price condemned him for a wasted life. How, he wondered, could such an insignificant man be in the position to bring him down?

From the morning he packed up and left his family's home in a mining town, Price was determined to be a big name on the college campus of 30,000 students. He enrolled under the name Price Logan, leaving the life and times of Walter Langdon to wither and rot. He never wrote or rode home again.

Price would be damned before he let Harry turn his life into a loss. He planned and plotted to be a winner and would die one. He needed a couple more years before stepping down as president and CEO of his company. He needed that time to be hailed as an astute businessman and lauded for a legacy of honesty, integrity, and immense charitable contributions. He wanted recognition in life as well as death.

He felt himself immortal. And he would live well on the extra millions stashed in a private account at a bank in the Cayman Islands, ill-gotten goods accumulated over the years by laundering drug money, then hiding it from the IRS.

He emptied his coffee cup, and the search through Harry's junk began again. It would be another six hours before all the contents of the van occupied one of the three piles. He was determined to go solo. He wasn't about to give someone else a chance to know the secret life of Price Logan.

Chapter 11

*M*arissa spotted Lauren first, then turned away from her sister for one last dab at the tears escaping her eyes. She put on a forced smile, turned back, and wrapped her arms around her best friend. First, a happy moment; the sky would fall soon enough.

Neither claimed the "big sister" advantage, even though Marissa was a day older. At any given moment, in any given situation, one of the sisters took the lead and the other followed. When the two hugged at the car rental counter, Marissa surrendered control of her emotions. A waterfall of despair and sadness raced down both cheeks.

Even if Lauren had asked her what was wrong, Marissa's brain was incapable of forming words. Lauren didn't ask; she just tightened her arms around her sister.

They had decided long ago to be there for one another. Lauren reminded herself that, back in college, both had pledged only one could have major turmoil at a time. Clearly, today Marissa's problem was Lauren's problem too. She put all thoughts of Harry's murder in a mental suitcase, shut It, and put it on a back shelf.

Lauren waited for Marissa to stop shaking. The two found their rental car and Lauren drove to a nearby park. She turned the motor off and sat quietly. Marissa would talk when she was ready.

"Dad called me last night," Marissa said, and the tears rained down her face once more. "I heard Mother crying in the background, but Dad wouldn't say anything except that it was vital that I come home as soon as I landed in Seattle. He said they needed to talk to me alone.

"Lauren, I can't face them alone. I need you to stay and hear whatever it is they have to tell me. Even if they ask, don't leave me. I'm frightened. I can't explain it, but it feels familiar. Something is wrong. Something is very wrong."

Lauren had been unofficially adopted by the Taylor clan when her only living relative and guardian had died unexpectedly of a heart attack. That was six years ago. She felt and had been treated like a Taylor since she had accepted their offer to join the family. Lauren was unsure why she was being left out of this seemingly ominous family discussion. It would affect her too, right? She didn't mention the slight she felt to Marissa, who was clearly unable to handle any more turmoil, real or imagined.

Lauren swallowed a big dose of selfishness, admitting to herself she had never felt so sad and alone. In the end, she wasn't really one of them. And they had closed ranks, leaving her outside the family circle.

Lauren handed Marissa another tissue and promised to stay by her side. "It may not be as bad as you imagine. You're famous for jumping to conclusions. Remember how I used to kid you that jumping to conclusions was the only daily exercise you got, remember?"

"Nice try, but Mom's just like you; she doesn't cry, you know that," Marissa said. "One of them is dying, probably Dad, and Mom will be lost without him." She began to sob again, and Lauren just let her cry until she ran out of tears and began to hiccup.

"Marissa, when's the last time you ate? I'm betting it was before dinner last night when Dad called you, right?"

Marissa wasn't hungry and lamented that this weekend was supposed to be a Taylor celebration. Instead, it felt more like an ending to the life she knew and loved. She had no more tears.

Lauren wondered what it was like to feel so deeply. She never cried, not when her parents died and not when Aunt Sarah died. Easier just to shut down and pretend you don't hurt.

Lauren did feel different this time; she could feel stirrings in her stomach. While Marissa gave way to tears, Lauren suppressed the need to vomit. She couldn't run away or shut down; her sister needed her. Lauren never broke a promise. She steadied herself, put the car in drive, and headed for home. Both were scared. Both were dealing in their own ways. Who's to say which was better?

The rental car pulled up at their parents' house, which sat at the top of a hill overlooking Puget Sound. The huge home had been in the Taylor family for several generations and was surrounded by an acre of tall trees with a rambling brook that ran every which direction before cascading over a boulder. The building was handsome, large and covered on the west side with floor-to-ceiling windows. Several garden doors poured out onto multi-tiered stone terraces.

Marissa had pictured her wedding here ever since she was a child. Almost happened that way too. A handful of years ago, she had planned the perfect wedding. Another sad remembrance for another day, she thought, grateful that it had ended before it really began. Her fiancé was tall and blond and laughed a lot. Turned out she was the punchline for a wandering Casanova. She thought she had picked a man who was a lot like her dad, but it didn't turn out that way.

That last thought, *Dad*, made her suck in her breath and steady her nerves. She was an adult, educated and on the way to a successful career. It was time for her to be the adult and be strong for her parents.

Lauren and Marissa locked arms and headed for the mahogany doors, steeled to slay whatever dragon reared its ugly head.

Chapter 12

*B*en Taylor was sitting in his favorite leather chair reading a newspaper. Joan Taylor stared out the window, trying to string words together she wasn't prepared to say out loud. She had convinced herself that this day would never come. She thought about it every year on her daughter's birthday. Not Marissa's actual birthday; instead, it would forever be celebrated on the date she and Ben brought their adopted daughter home.

Joan had agreed to tell Marissa about the adoption, but only after Ben promised that no details of the abuse and murder be revealed. They agreed the right time would be when Marissa came to Seattle for the couple's anniversary party.

Joan remembered the early days when they first brought Marissa home. The tot cried a lot those first weeks, jolted awake from a deep slumber by nightmares. The weekly traumas always started with a whimper and ended with inconsolable sobs. Joan cursed the man who had done this to her, swore she would never let him near the child again.

Not that it could ever happen. The birth father was serving a life sentence for killing his wife during a drunken rage. Ben first met the abusive man when the court tapped him to serve as defense attorney in the case, State of Illinois versus Earl Malone Watson.

There was never any doubt that Watson had abused his wife on numerous occasions. Susan Watson had come to the emergency room where Joan worked as a nurse. This visit would be Susan's third and final cry for help. This time, neither stitches nor bandages could repair the damage her husband had inflicted.

Joan and Susan had talked when the battered wife showed up in the emergency room less than two months earlier. She staggered in holding her young daughter in her left arm; the other arm dangled, broken and bruised. Joan held the child and tried comforting her while the doctor examined her mother.

Susan defended her husband, saying he was kind most of the time and took care of the young family. She had come from poverty and remained convinced that hunger and homelessness were worse than suffering a few beatings. She only wished her daughter didn't have to hear and see all the violence. She wanted more for Marie. She prayed for a life of love and safety for her baby, a life Susan could never offer her much-loved child.

Marie nuzzled her face into Joan's ample bosom and fell asleep. Joan kissed little Marie's forehead and told Susan how lucky she was to have such a wonderful child. The nurse encouraged her patient to get away from her husband, but the young wife couldn't and wouldn't leave him.

They talked for hours. Susan asked Joan how many children she had; the nurse shook her head and told her none, but maybe soon. Ben and Joan were on waiting lists at several adoption agencies.

On the way out of the ER, Susan folded a note and was about to ask the woman at the desk to put it in her medical file when a ringing phone cut the conversation short. Her attention averted, Susan used the opportunity to slip the note under a paper clip inside her medical folder. The note was discovered the night her medical file was pulled and stamped "deceased."

Susan that last night had arrived by ambulance, more dead than alive. If Susan had opened her eyes, she would have seen Joan holding her hand and promising that everything would be all right. The young mother never opened her eyes; everything wasn't all right. Not for her, but maybe for little Marie.

Ben and Joan talked about that night from time to time. They remembered the court's decision to honor Susan Watson's final written request. She wanted Joan Taylor to be her daughter's mother.

Little Marie Watson entered the judge's chamber; Marissa Taylor walked out holding hands with Ben and Joan Taylor. The little girl giggled and skipped, dropping her weight so her parents could swing her tiny body.

The Taylors decided there was too much history for the young girl to ever make her way through school without the past making a normal childhood impossible. The family of three packed up and moved from Chicago to Ben's family home in Seattle before Marissa's third birthday.

That was more than two decades ago, and today was a day of remembering and revealing. Joan didn't know how her daughter would react. *Her* daughter, she repeated to herself, praying that God would help Marissa forgive her.

But, most importantly, Joan didn't want her daughter to remember her childhood traumas. And she resented having to share her role as "mother" with Susan, which only made Joan feel small and selfish.

Marissa and Lauren walked into the den, arm-in-arm, and dispensed with the usual greetings, instead wanting to know details.

"Mom, Dad, you're scaring me. Please, talk to us," Marissa said.

Ben looked at Lauren and asked her to wait outside while they had a private conversation with their daughter. But Marissa's grip tightened; she insisted that the whole family should hear whatever it was they needed to tell her.

Ben looked at Joan; Joan turned to look at Lauren; then they all stared at Marissa. Ben shrugged his shoulders and agreed that Lauren should stay, telling Joan that maybe it was better if Marissa had Lauren there.

The story unfolded with Joan telling Marissa how dear she was, that a mother would always protect her daughter the same as a mommy grizzly bear protects her cub.

Marissa and Lauren sat on the sofa, wondering what their mom was so desperately trying *not* to tell them.

"Your mother and I adopted you when you were very young, almost three."

The two young women sat at the edge of the sofa, listening but not speaking. Ben recounted the death of her birth mother, and the blessed call they got from the adoption agency telling them they had a daughter.

Then Ben told her about the adoption, made possible by a handwritten note Susan Watson placed in the hospital's medical folder. "I met your mother when she was a patient at the hospital,"

Joan said, "and we got to know one another. When she died, the hospital found a note in the file asking that I be your new mother. I saved the note.

"Every year we wondered if it was time to tell you, but you had grown out of the nightmare stage and began to look to me for comfort," Joan said. "Perhaps we were wrong. You grew into such a happy child and blossomed as a teenager, and those are some tough years. Then you went back to Illinois for college and we thought it was time.

"This is on me, not your dad. He always thought we should tell you on your eighteenth birthday. I prayed this day would never come. I never wanted you to know."

Ben reached for his daughter's hand and squeezed it. She looked up at her father and asked him if there was something else he needed to tell her.

"You're not going to be easy on us, are you?" Ben said. "Okay, go ahead with whatever it is you need to say to us. We deserve it."

"What you deserve is my everlasting love and respect for the people you are," she said. "I'm stunned, maybe too stunned and confused to talk about this. Turns out we have more in common than we thought," she said, turning to face Lauren. "Seems Mom and Dad adopted both of us."

She wasn't being snide and not trying to be funny. What came out of her mouth next was the first thought that formed in her head.

"What did my birth mother name me?" Marissa asked.

"Marie," she told her daughter. "Your mother named you Marie."

Marissa got up from the sofa and headed for the terrace doors. She asked her father to come for a walk, adding, "Let's not talk. I just need to feel your love and strength."

She whispered to Lauren to sit with her mom and just let her talk. Her mom always needed to talk things out, but Marissa needed quiet and the calming scent of the trees and wind blowing off the water below. And she needed strength from her father because inside she felt frightened.

She didn't know who or what caused fear to surround her. She felt like jelly inside and needed the steady comfort in the company of the only father she knew or wanted, Benjamin Thomas Taylor.

Chapter 13

Marissa and her father walked in silence until they reached a bench at the end of a cobbled path overlooking Puget Sound. The expression on her father's face was foreign to her. Not anger, more like defeat. She hadn't really digested the past half hour, and she suspected there was more.

Suddenly, her legs felt wobbly. Marissa didn't know if she could hear any more, but his first words were alarming. She sat down on the bench and inhaled the salt air, filling her lungs to capacity. She let the air out slowly and looked up at her father.

"There is something else you need to know, something your mother doesn't know. It's the only thing I've ever done behind her back," Ben told his daughter. "Let me start at the beginning; then maybe you will understand some of the decisions your mother and I made and the one decision I made without your mother's knowledge or consent."

She told her dad that nothing he could say would make her love him less. Ben Taylor was the only dad she had ever known, the only father who had loved her unconditionally, and that was that. Case closed, she told him.

"You've been trained better than that," he told her. "You can't really make a decision without hearing all the facts. I don't expect any of this to change our relationship or make you feel less loved or cherished. I think you have a right to know details of your life from the moment you were born. Your mother disagreed. In thirty years of marriage, this is the only subject where we have agreed to disagree. I let her have her way; maybe that was a mistake."

Marissa squeezed her father's hand and bowed her head: "Okay, Dad, start at the beginning."

He told her that she was born July 4, 1954, in Chicago, to Earl and Susan Watson. Her mother was 19 at the time; her father was 21. They named their only child Marie Watson.

He started to tread lightly with details when his daughter reminded him that he promised to tell the truth, the whole truth, no matter how disturbing. Ben reluctantly agreed.

"Your mother loved you so much, and in the end, she died trying to protect you," he said. "Mom, your adopted mother, was a nurse in the emergency room, which is where the two met. Susan took an immediate liking to Joan, and it ran both ways. Joan tried to reason with her, told her to take you and run away. But Susan couldn't bring herself to do that. I think Susan stayed because she had no way of supporting the two of you. She told Joan that Earl was a good provider and a decent husband most of the time; it was the alcohol that made him mean.

"Your father was an alcoholic and never managed to hold a steady job. He was a petty thief, mainly lifting wallets for cash to buy booze and place bets. Your mom thought he had a job, but when she found a couple of wallets in the trash, she confronted him. Earl had been drinking all day and reacted violently when Susan called him a petty thief."

Ben told his daughter that Earl had admitted details of their final argument and blamed his wife for provoking him. He insisted that she had driven him to kill her.

"I was assigned by the courts to defend him. Our firm did a certain amount of pro bono work and I was drafted for the defense," Ben said. "I didn't like your father at first, but after the trial I visited him when he was sober. I saw a different side and wanted to know more about this man so if you ever wanted to know more, I could give you some answers."

Ben told her some of Earl's childhood history, about the abuse and years in foster homes until he ran away at age 16. "The man believed that hitting and screaming was just the way families settled disagreements. Sobriety and counseling had made a dent in his thinking, and he figured he had a whole lifetime to repent. His only regret was that he would never leave prison, never be able to ask for your forgiveness."

Ben told her the only time he saw the prisoner cry was when he talked about what would happen to his only daughter, Marie.

"Your parents were arguing when you walked in the room and you started crying. He raised his hand, but your mother stepped between the two of you and blocked his fist. The more he beat her, the louder you screamed. A neighbor heard the commotion and called the police."

Marissa didn't know what to feel. So many emotions came and went: anger, pity, love for Susan Watson, hate for Earl Watson, and finally fear for the defenseless child hiding somewhere inside her.

"We pieced all of this together from what the neighbors told us and from your father's confession," Ben told Marissa. "He pleaded guilty but not sorry. Told the judge his wife got what she deserved, and the judge was as unforgiving as your father."

Ben saw Earl a few more times while he was in prison but never mentioned the note Susan had written and placed for safekeeping in her medical file at the hospital.

Ben never told Earl that he and his wife were in the process of formally adopting his only daughter. The same judge who had sentenced Earl to life signed off on the adoption and sealed the records.

Earl asked for a photo of little Marie, and Ben saw no harm. It was unlikely that Earl would ever see the outside of a prison cell. The judge told him as much and vowed to make sure Earl would stay in prison for the rest of his life.

On Marissa's 16th birthday, Ben figured no harm in sending Earl an updated picture of his daughter. Anonymously, of course, with no return address. He mailed it to a friend at his old Chicago law firm. He instructed Tom Kromer to forward the sealed envelope inside so it would have a local postmark.

The law firm had instructions to forward all inquiries about the family to Kromer, the senior partner who had hired Ben as a law clerk and then kept him on after he passed the bar. Kromer was the only person who knew the family had relocated in Seattle. The new city meant a fresh start for all three Taylors, and they flourished in their new surroundings.

Ben received notification that Earl Watson was going to be released from prison in early December but decided that Joan didn't need to know. He was surprised to learn that the ex-con visited his old office to look him up; he had counted on never seeing the man again. His soft heart and empathy for another father was about to blow up in his face. Marissa, at 25, looked pretty much the same as when she was sixteen. If their paths crossed, Watson would easily make the connection.

The private garden talk between Ben and Marissa would have shocked Joan, and the hurt would be deep and lasting. She would feel betrayed. He was determined that she never find out about the picture he had sent to Earl Watson.

The Seattle rains grew from a drizzle to a downpour, sending father and daughter running back into the house. It was the first time either had laughed all day. Joan opened the patio doors wide and held two towels in her arms.

Ben figured he had at least a week before Earl could find him, plenty of time not to spoil this anniversary weekend. He would suggest that Marissa take a vacation and spend it with Lauren in Santa Vista. Both young women worked too hard, he told himself, and a week at the beach was just the solution to a problem neither was aware of.

Then he put his plan into words, asking Lauren to invite Marissa for a week's stay at the beach to give her time to digest and talk about all that had occurred the past couple hours.

"She needs you, Lauren," Ben told her. "Don't take no for an answer."

"And there's nothing more you want to tell me," Lauren whispered. "We're a lot alike and I can read your face. Something's wrong. If you want to talk, I'm here. Just no more secrets, promise?"

Ben took Lauren's hands in his, told her he loved her, and added, "You've asked me for a promise that I'm unable to keep. Soon I will honor that request, just not today."

"It's important that Marissa fly out with me on Monday, isn't it?"

"Yes, Lauren, very important." Suddenly, Lauren felt frightened for Ben, and a cold shadow breezed through her soul. Lauren promised her father that Marissa would be on the plane to Santa Vista with her. And then she made him promise to call if he needed her.

Chapter 14

E arl Malone Watson walked out of state prison shortly after eleven o'clock on a December morning in 1979, a crisp hundred-dollar bill in his new suit pocket and a hunger for sausage pizza. None of that cheese-baked-on-dough prison crap served Fridays; he yearned for the same pizza he and Susan enjoyed Sunday afternoons at Angelini's on West Lawrence. All he could think about was ice-cold draft beer and sausage pizza, no cheese.

Watson never imagined this day, but new laws had forced judges to reexamine and reduce life sentences on a case-by-case basis. The prison board said he was rehabilitated. Watson was assigned a parole officer and warned not to leave the city. The warden shook his hand and wished him well.

He waited for the clang of the iron gates before he allowed himself to feel the freedom. Watson raised his hand, whistled for a cab. He climbed in and barked out the address; first on his list was pizza and cold beer. He felt the knots in his body relax and then tense again as the idea of this newfound freedom weighed heavy in his gut.

Watson stared out the taxi windows on the long ride from past to present, and the quarter-century lapse catapulted him into a new and strange world. Until this moment, his only glimpse of the outside world was through a television set bolted to the ceiling in the prison's rec room. Black and white, and censored.

The taxi braked in front of a liquor store, and the middle-aged man in the fresh suit offered the $100 bill as payment. The cabbie refused, saying the ride was a gift and he wished the man peace and happiness. He knew from personal experience that the road in front of this ex-con was filled with potholes; he knew because he had walked in this man's shoes and only survived with help from strangers. He, like most cons, had used his friends until there was no more to give. He liked being the one extending the helping hand. It felt good and left him whistling as he pulled away from the curb and headed north.

Watson stuffed the bill back in his pocket and was pleased that Angelini's looked pretty much the same. He headed for the liquor store door, the sole entry to the adjoining pizza parlor. He went inside and walked through aisles crammed with glass bottles of vodka, gin, rum, tequila, and whiskey. He passed through a door leading to the familiar restaurant and slipped into a red vinyl booth.

He opened the menu, but it was all wrong; he didn't see what he craved. Watson caught the attention of a nearby waitress, ordered a sausage pizza with no cheese and any brew on tap. She smiled. "Been awhile since you've been here. The pizza you want is old school, don't get many requests for sausage only. Be right back with your beer."

The glass was icy, the beer just as cold. He picked up the glass and brought it to his lips but didn't take a sip. He shivered, put the glass down, and rubbed his hands for warmth.

What was he thinking? he wondered. Prison had been hard, but it had straightened out his thinking. He had been wrong to abuse his wife. Alcohol didn't excuse his behavior. It took him several years to figure that out.

Suddenly, the starting point for the rest of his life became very clear. Watson called the waitress over, asked her to take the beer away and bring water without ice. He made the decision not to drink until he had made amends to his daughter. His past behavior left a bitter taste in his mouth that no beer, no matter how good, could wash away. Maybe he would drink another day, maybe not. Nothing that needed to be decided now, he told himself.

Watson promised himself he would find his daughter and apologize for the grief he had caused her. He had received a picture of her on her 16th birthday, an anonymous gift, and he had taped it to the cell wall nearest to his pillow. There was no note, no return address, just a photo of the daughter he had betrayed in a rage of anger. Fits of anger, he reminded himself, uncontrolled rage that played itself out over several years.

The deadly outcome had been only a matter of time. He couldn't remember what his dead wife looked like, but he remembered her laugh, the way she would throw her head back and laugh so hard her whole body shook. Their only daughter looked more like him than Susan. Marie got his green eyes and dishwater blonde hair. They shared a petite nose and lean body.

Watson was grateful to the couple who had adopted his daughter and figured the picture was a gift from God, rewarding him for so many years of sobriety. But he wanted more — he wanted to see her and ask for her forgiveness. He meant to find her. In the beginning, he planned just to look at her from afar. But as the years rolled by, he needed more and intended to seek out the young lawyer who had represented him to see if he would help the father find his daughter.

Watson made a mental note to stop by the firm and thank him. Ben Taylor was the man's name. The firm of Kromer, Somme and Thornton wasn't far from the pizza restaurant where he sat contemplating his next moves. Strange not having anyone to tell him when to eat, when to sleep, and what to think.

He decided to finish every morsel of sausage, then walk along Lakefront Trail. More than any other person, place, or thing, Watson missed the smell of the waterfront near Monroe Harbor. This was the place where he could lose himself and daydream about a life beyond his reach, the same place his mind escaped when prison life sucked his spirit dry.

Watson looked down at his hands, fidgeted, and felt deflated. A sudden breeze from the lake felt like a slap in the face. Reality had invaded his place of escape; the bench by the lake no longer brought him comfort.

The sun was releasing the last of its heat before winter skies extinguished its glow. For the first time, on his first day of freedom, Earl Watson realized he was on his own, and not in a good way. He reached in his pocket and counted three twenties, two sawbucks, and two quarters. He shivered, closed his coat tight around his lean body, and headed inland to find a place to begin another chapter of his life. This one, he hoped, would have a happier ending.

Chapter 15

*I*f Watson could have written the script for the life he was enjoying on his first day of freedom, he would have awarded himself five stars. It all seemed so unreal, both the dread of the unknown in the days before his release and the hours since he walked out of prison a free man.

The ex-con returned to his bench by the lake just to sit and inhale the smell and taste of freedom. And to dream one last dream. Marie. Where was his sweet daughter? Was she happy? Did she think about him often or even at all?

And, most of all, would Marie forgive him and let her father be a part of the rest of her life? He wondered if he had grandchildren. If he did, he hoped he would have another chance to set things right. Time to find out, he told himself. He took a deep breath and headed for the only logical place to begin his search.

It was late afternoon when Watson pushed open the doors of the law firm that had played such a pivotal part in his life so many years ago. Everything was different, including the name of a new partner engraved in gold lettering and added to the huge walnut office doors.

The stranger caught the attention and admiration of the receptionist. *Tall, lean, and ruggedly handsome, maybe late forties, early fifties,* she thought. And she wondered if he was single, noticing no gold band on his ring finger.

Watson smiled as he approached the receptionist. She was staring intently, maybe even flirting a bit. Lots of women came on to him many years ago, and he never minded because there was always something in it for him too. He smiled back, and his light green eyes mesmerized the middle-aged woman. His voice was deep and soft at the same time.

"I'd like to see Ben Taylor," he told her.

She looked puzzled and replied that no one by that name worked at the firm. No Ben Taylor, but a lawyer named Marissa Taylor was on staff, she told him. The conversation suddenly was cut short by senior partner Tom Kromer, who abducted the conversation mid-flirt.

"You know who I am, don't you?" Watson said, staring at Kromer. "I'm Earl Watson and I'm not here to make trouble. I just wanted to talk to Ben Taylor. Ask him some questions about my daughter."

Kromer shrugged nonchalantly, said Taylor had left the firm a year after the murder trial to set up a private practice in Boston. The secretary started to say something when Kromer's glare forced her to swallow the rest of her sentence.

"We can't help you here, so let me show you to the door, Mr. Watson." Kromer turned on his heels and made a straight path toward the confused receptionist. His voice was low and angry. "What did you say to him?"

"He was looking for Ben Taylor and I told him there was no one here by that name," she said, looking down at her lap. "Just that there was a Marissa Taylor but that she wasn't here, left for Seattle. That's all."

Her answer was met with a groan, then several "Oh my Gods." Kromer made a beeline for his private office and slammed the door. He had to call Ben in Seattle to warn him. Watson was free and was probably looking to find his daughter — Ben's adopted daughter, Marissa Taylor.

The line was busy. Kromer had a flight to catch for meetings with a client in New York, but he grabbed an envelope, stuffed some hundreds inside, and sealed it shut. On his way out the door, he handed it to the receptionist without explanation. Two weeks' pay; her services were no longer needed. She watched Kromer storm out; she was angrier than puzzled. What the hell just happened?

Kromer planned to call his old friend first thing the next day. He placed the call early morning on Saturday. Joan Taylor was on the other end of the line and assumed the call was for Marissa. She offered to take a message or have her daughter return the call, but Kromer interrupted and told her he needed to talk with Ben. In a forced casual voice, he added, "Important, but not urgent. Just have him call me."

Joan was blissfully unaware of the impending storm headed her family's way. Her husband was all too aware after his conversation with Kromer an hour later. Ben knew he was obligated to tell Marissa about her past to arm her with the facts if, *no*, when Earl Watson confronted her.

Kromer apologized for the receptionist's talk with Watson, adding, "She told him Marissa was on holiday with her parents in Seattle. I interrupted the conversation and showed him out. But I think he's headed your way. Can't know if he's made the connection about Marissa being Marie. Sorry, Ben, so sorry. I thought you should know he came to the office."

Chapter 16

auren telephoned airline reservations to book a flight for Marissa before she had formulated a plan to get her sister to travel south instead of returning to Chicago. Booking another ticket would be easier, she thought. Turned out, not so much. Her ten o'clock flight was booked solid, forcing her to cancel her reservation and rebook two seats on a plane leaving two hours earlier.

Now for the hard part—convincing Marissa to take some time off. She laughed at her own stupidity. She didn't need a plan, she needed a plot. While Lauren led with her wit, Marissa followed her heart. Lauren had to make Marissa think she was needed, that her sister was in some unspoken trouble. There was more fact than fiction in her thinking, something Lauren would find out in the next week as trouble came looking for her. But for the moment, an unnamed trouble only existed in the fertile mind of the young journalist.

Lauren and Marissa decided to go out, leaving their parents to rest before the anniversary gala later that night at the country club. Sipping glasses of chardonnay at a favorite bistro, they toasted their good fortune at being loved and cherished by Ben and Joan Taylor. The ease of the glasses clinking belied their forced smiles. Physically they were in the same place; mentally, time and space put them at odds.

Marissa was back in the garden, her memory replaying Ben's pained confession. She didn't want to think or feel. She needed an escape from reality. Her heart hurt but she wasn't ready to deal or heal. Part of her knew she had to feel the pain; the child in her wanted to hide under the bed covers. She wondered why that was her usual go-to solution when life overwhelmed her. Marissa couldn't remember ever doing anything else when disaster painted her world in scary colors. Always the same, always black and blue. She wondered but wasn't ready to search for answers, afraid she might find them. A part of her, the child in her, screamed for her to run and hide.

Lauren hadn't a clue what Marissa was thinking or feeling. She began to execute her plan to convince Marissa to come for a visit and stay a while. Lauren put on her best pained expression and figured Marissa would ask for details, then come up with a rescue plan. It clearly wasn't working; she was being ignored. Lauren tried a different tact.

"I think I saw a murder." The halting words slipped from Lauren's lips and she waited for the expected overreaction from her sister. Nothing. "I could be wrong, but I'm not," she continued, unsure of what to say next if Marissa didn't scream for details.

"Not what?" Marissa said, half listening. Marissa wanted to tell Lauren about the conversation with her father but felt it would be a betrayal to her mother. And to her father? Had she promised Ben not to tell Lauren? She couldn't remember. All she felt was sad. She wanted to go somewhere and think, some place away from the routine. Some place, just not back to Chicago.

"How would you feel about having a house guest for a week?" Marissa said. "I think I need a vacation."

Lauren stared at her sister and felt a stabbing pain in her heart. Marissa was clearly the one in need; an unspoken trouble veiled her face. She had only seen this once before, the night that Marissa's heart had been damaged irreparably. She had held Marissa close and coached her to breathe in and out. In and out. She held her for hours while Marissa sobbed.

It was their senior year in college and Marissa had expected graduation to be followed by her wedding. There *was* a wedding. Alan's wedding. The nuptials read Alan Benning and Pamela Newell.

Marissa had been betrayed by a man she had trusted without a doubt. His doubts led him into the arms of another woman, figuring a last fling before a lifetime of commitment could do no harm. The distance between Chicago and Boston made him cocky, no chance he'd be caught. But his virility and lack of protection had caused his life to take a 180-degree tumble. Pamela and Alan, bride and groom in June, mother and father by Christmas. It took nearly a year for Marissa not to care. It took another year before she reluctantly agreed to go on a date.

Lauren had never been serious about one man. Infatuation was her pleasure. She would love them and leave them, lots of them. Marissa was tolerant of her friend's promiscuity but stayed on the sidelines of love. She placed all her time and energy into law school and had spent summers working at women's shelters. Later, most of her caseloads involved family law. When people would ask what attracted her to this field, she would say that having "loving parents and a blessed childhood" made her want to give back. And she believed it.

So much history; the two women had been there for one another during good times and bad times. Lauren remembered the look on

Ben's face earlier that day, her promise to him about Santa Vista and the not knowing of secrets that had so obviously changed Marissa's world.

Lauren reached across the table and took Marissa's hand in hers. She gave it a squeeze and told her that arrangements for her to come back to Santa Vista had already been done.

And then she lied, "I knew you needed me."

There was no self-satisfaction in the lie, no gloating, only a knowing that she hadn't felt since her aunt Sarah had put her arms around her and promised everything would be all right. This time it was her turn to make sure everything would be all right. Ben could count on her; Marissa too, without a doubt.

The two hugged. Marissa took a deep breath and promised that this anniversary would be one for the books. They left for home to shower and dress for the fancy night of dining and dancing. Neither had a date. Nothing new there.

Chapter 17

A gust of cold air woke Lauren early Monday morning, sending a shiver racing up her spine and back until the hairs on her neck stood at attention. She pulled the down comforter over her head. Trouble was heading her way, a darkness with no name, sweeping nearer and nearer. Vague and haunting, cold as death.

She wondered, had it followed her here from Santa Vista or had it been festering and waiting for her arrival in Seattle?

Lauren threw back the warm bedding and stood up naked, staring into space and daring the unknown to come close and identify itself. She braced herself for the battle, challenging trouble to confront her head-on. "Right now," she commanded. But the silence refused to reveal itself.

She threw on jeans, a hooded sweatshirt, and knotted her running shoes. She stopped at the doorway and spun around. Nothing. She pulled open the closet and drawers, throwing the contents on the unmade bed. She wadded her party dress, panty hose, and pajamas around her black suede pumps, then tossed the bundle into a denim carry-on bag. Short flight, she figured, everything was headed for the laundry anyway.

Lauren dropped the bag near the front door and headed out for a jog by the water. The early morning fog swallowed her whole and afforded her a sense of invulnerability and safety.

Her mind raced to assemble the bits and pieces of a puzzle, but the huge pile left her clueless. It was like someone had handed her a 500-piece jigsaw without a picture box.

While her body moved, her mind was occupied sorting out the few facts she had been told, bits and pieces she overheard and some she had observed. She started at the beginning, Saturday, when anticipation for a 30th gala was on everyone's mind.

Lauren had planned to talk about the possible murder she had witnessed the day after the party. Saturday was reserved for good thoughts and unquestioning love.

The day took a strange turn when Ben answered a long-distance telephone call. When he came back into the sun room, Ben's mood, his voice, and his manner were thinly veiled with a shrug and a smile. The thing was, Lauren saw through it the moment their eyes connected. She was a lot like the man who called her his adopted daughter.

Pain washed off the disguise he wore for show. Joan didn't notice; neither did Marissa. Just Lauren. When her face expressed concern, he shook his head and mouthed the word "later." His lips smiled but his heart wasn't buying any of it. Lauren and Marissa sat waiting for conversation to begin.

Looking back, Lauren realized she didn't know who was on the other end of the phone, why he or she called, or why it shook Ben to the core.

His wife didn't notice because she was lost in self-talk, practicing the words she would use to tell Marissa about a past she and Ben had guarded with secrecy for more than two decades. The conversation was a practiced script narrated by Joan. Marissa was quiet at first, and then her curiosity begged for details about her birth parents. Joan pleaded ignorance; she had no information to offer her daughter because it was a closed adoption. Joan added that she was glad not to know. She wanted to be the only mother, not the adopted parent.

Ben and Marissa headed outside for a father-daughter talk while Lauren kept up a one-sided conversation with Joan. Ben told Marissa what Joan had forbidden: He told her the details about years of abuse which led to the murder of her mother and a life sentence without parole for the husband.

A half hour later, Ben and Marissa ran inside, clothes drenched from a sudden afternoon downpour. Lauren realized her friend had been crying; Marissa just shook her head when Lauren asked her what was wrong. All she would say was "Later."

Soon, they would be sitting side-by-side on an airplane heading south and the journalist would have her curiosity sated. Joan Taylor was glad to see her girls make plans to spend some time together.

The party had been attended by local politicians, bankers, lawyers, and old friends. There were so many toasts — both Ben and Joan drank more in one night than they had in the last month. Marissa was up early and left the house to meet old friends for shopping and a late Sunday brunch. Dinner was light, both in fare and conversation.

Monday morning, the two women drove to the airport in silence. Clearly Marissa wasn't ready to talk. She settled in the passenger's seat and stared at the raindrops pelting the windshield. If she could have put her feelings into words, Marissa would have confessed it seemed she was a visitor in a strange world. She didn't know what to say or do or how to feel or what to think. She needed to get to Santa Vista with Lauren and talk the whole thing out in private.

The quiet allowed Lauren to revisit the days before she left for Seattle. She found herself smiling about the idea of being home, curled up on the stuffed sofa with a big red dog named Charlee Bear. She had never had a pet of her own, not even a goldfish, but the idea of having someone to talk to who wouldn't talk back made her smile.

They dropped the rental car off and climbed aboard a crowded shuttle for the few blocks to the airport. The small bus pulled up on the opposite side of the street, the doors flipped open, and Lauren sprinted for cover.

Chapter 18

*L*auren blindly dashed from the bus for dry cover. A yellow cab pulled up behind the bus, and the lone passenger set off full-speed, targeting the same plot of dry sidewalk. Marissa saw the impending disaster and yelled at Lauren, but her voice was no match for the mix of rain on asphalt, revving engines, and honking cars.

She watched as the two bodies collided, merged, and plunged into the fast-moving water. A muddy runoff swirled around Lauren and the tall man. Both popped up as fast as they plummeted, but the water damage was done. Soaked and shivering, both offered apologies while shaking off excess water. He asked if she was okay while she checked to see if he was hurt. Apologies were offered and accepted by both parties, and then he disappeared into the cavernous terminal.

Marissa caught up with Lauren and they took off running before the San Francisco flight left them standing at the gate. Heavy traffic and long lines at the rental car agency cut out precious minutes allocated for coffee and a bathroom break before boarding. They were the last two boarding before the cabin door was slammed and secured.

The women found their seats mid-plane. Lauren reached for a blanket to wrap around her wet jeans, then grabbed a second blanket and a pillow before scooting to the window seat. Marissa took the aisle seat, reached for the seat belt, and was ready to settle back when she heard a man's voice informing her that she was sitting in his seat. She looked up and started chuckling. It was the same man who had collided with Lauren outside the terminal. He stood clenching a fistful of paper napkins, rubbing his left arm.

"Sorry," she said, "would you like to sit next to my friend? I believe you two have met." Her last words trailed off as her eyes scanned the handsome man with beautiful green eyes. She pushed into the middle seat and offered the man Lauren's second blanket. "This should help warm you. I'm Marissa, my friend is Lauren. Glad neither of you is hurt. That was some fall you took."

"Tower. My name is Tower," he offered. "This has been a bad day all around, bad week, bad month. I'm not usually this grumpy, but I'm cold, tired, and heading someplace I don't want to go."

Marissa decided it was best to read and leave the man alone. She pulled out a magazine, eyes scanning the contents when she heard his offer of thanks for the blanket.

"You're welcome," Lauren said, leaning over her friend, "and if you don't want to go to San Francisco, why didn't you just say no and not go?"

He snorted; just looking at the woman made his mood change, despite his commitment to stay grumpy.

"Ignore her," Marissa said. "Lauren is a newspaper reporter and she thinks everyone's business is her business. Means well, she just can't help being nosy."

"And you, Marissa, what is it you do?" he asked.

"If you're in any kind of trouble, shell out a retainer fee before you say a word." Lauren laughed. "Client-attorney privilege and all that."

"I'm a family attorney, and my passion is helping protect children from abusive parents." Marissa punctuated her remarks as if she had just rendered a verdict. Guilty. She felt an unknown sadness sweep over her spirit and realized her eyes were filling with water. Tears of guilt? Fear? Anger at herself or frustration in not knowing about her early years of abuse?

She wondered if some part of her had remembered details of the abuse she endured as a child. Clearly, the man who had killed her mother spilled his uncontrolled anger on her too. Could that be why she had chosen to do this work with such a vengeance? What childhood memories lay buried deep in her past? All three sighed and shivered — Tower and Lauren from damp clothes; Marissa from an ominous shadow clawing at her soul to be set free.

Tower and Lauren were chatting when Marissa's attention snapped back to the present. They were laughing, hands warming wrapped around paper cups filled with steaming liquid. She wondered how long she had been mentally absent. Marissa's eyes scanned the aisle where she spotted the beverage cart two rows aft. She pushed the call button and requested soda with ice. She put the cup to her lips and listened while the conversation continued without her.

Marissa forced a change in her thoughts, instead concentrating on the emerald green eyes she had spotted earlier. She desperately wanted to sneak another peek to confirm their intensity, but she was shy and blushed easily. What she wouldn't give to be more like

Lauren. World be damned, if you had something to say, it was out in the open. That was Lauren. Marissa sipped life; Lauren gulped.

The two women often giggled that it balanced out and, combined, they equaled one normal person. Boring, but normal.

Lauren poked Marissa in the ribs to get her to join the conversation. "What do you know, Tower is headed for Santa Vista after a meeting in San Francisco. Should we invite him over?"

Marissa's face turned scarlet. "Sure, whatever you think," she said, turning

to Tower. "Lauren has an apartment on the beach, so come by for lunch and we can picnic near the surf. I plan to become a beach bum for the week before I return to Chicago.

"Emerald green," Marissa heard herself saying out loud, choking on an apology for being so forward.

"A lot of folks say that about my eyes," Tower said. "Same for you, huh? But you are aware that your eyes are the most unusual shade of green, so light, almost translucent. First thing people notice, and it bothers you?"

He made her laugh. Marissa was guilty of the very thing she condemned in most people when they first met her—focusing on her aqua-green eyes, or sea-foam green, or peridot. People were mesmerized by her eyes and now she was doing the same thing to this stranger.

Lost in thought again, Marissa's mind raced to find answers to questions she had never really wondered about, not really, or had she? Joan's eyes were mocha; Ben's eyes were grizzly brown, his body big and bold. Everyone had mahogany hair, thick and straight; her curly locks were sandy blond.

Before Saturday, she believed she was exactly like her parents. Now, she didn't know what to believe. Or feel. Not so much about her parents — she loved them unconditionally. It was about the nightmares that haunted her.

As Marissa grew from child to adolescent, the nightmares were replaced with a deep desire to help children facing abuse and abandonment. She was determined to become a lawyer, just like her dad.

Vivid dreams started to haunt her again a few years back, particularly during the discovery phase at the start of each new case. Marissa attributed her restless nights to the natural reaction after hearing horror stories from her youngest clients about what they had seen and endured. So much abuse and heartache, and always fearful the next beating would be worse than the one before.

She was jolted back to the present by the thud of the landing gear as it dropped and locked. She gathered her thoughts and her belongings and sat waiting for whatever came next.

Tower was thinking about his future, both short term and long term. He knew he was going to resign from the FBI after he finished this last assignment. He decided Santa Vista was as good a place as any to plan his next career move.

Lauren scribbled her address and phone number and passed it to Tower with a promise to find out if the furnished cottage near her cottage was still available for a short rental. He liked the idea of staying near the beach, waking up to the smell of saltwater, jogging on the boardwalk, and toasting sunsets with a bottle of beer. Tower smiled at both women, then bounded from the plane.

"What just happened," Marissa demanded. "Is there something going on I should know about?"

"He was flirting with you," Lauren said. "Didn't you pick up on that? What's wrong with you, girl? Forget it, we'll get some wine, crash on my overstuffed couch with Charlee Bear, and talk. Clearly, you need to put some words to the thoughts and feelings swirling inside your head."

Chapter 19

The meter flipped off as the cab pulled up to the Ocean View cottages. Marissa stepped out of the car and filled her lungs with air, stretched, and congratulated herself for talking Lauren into letting her crash here for a week or so. Deep down, she knew Lauren wouldn't mind; she'd insist if she had any inkling about the turmoil locked inside her.

"Can't wait for you to meet Charlee Bear. He came with the cottage and is as comfortable as the overstuffed sofa," Lauren chatted, placing a $20 bill in the cabbie's palm.

"Go through the gate and it's the third cottage on the left, number three." She tossed her keys to Marissa and headed for Betty's house to let her know she was back. And to collect Charlee.

The dog had only been in her life a few days, but Lauren surprised herself at just how much she missed the big galoot. Unusual, she thought. She made a point of not attaching herself to places or things. She had been disappointed too many times. The only constant was change; and she carried her emotional baggage packed, no longer dreading what came next but always ready to move on. She didn't know that this core belief was about to be shaken down to its very roots.

"The key fits, but the place is empty, no couch, no bed, no refrigerator," Marissa called out. "Did I get the wrong place?"

Lauren's shot back a puzzled look, turned and rushed inside the cottage door. It took a second to register, but then her confusion erupted into anger. Nothing, not even the welcome mat. Empty, as empty as the sinking feeling in her stomach. She marched to the manager's cottage and pounded on the door, ready to fight for the furnished apartment she had been promised.

Billy Myers was guzzling a beer, his eyes on a sports game blaring on the TV. He was not happy about the intrusion, and his face said so. He uttered a "WHAT do you want," more accusation than inquiry, "on MY day off."

Lauren put her foot in the door as he was about to slam it shut. He pushed on the door, punctuating his determination to get back to his recliner, beer, and TV. Lauren slipped her body through the growing crack, determined to confront the man.

"What I want is for you to keep the promise you made to me! I signed a contract for a furnished apartment, so why did you take everything out? Even the refrigerator, damn it."

His face contorted into anger. He demanded to know what the hell she was talking about.

"The place is empty, and we agreed I could keep the furniture. That's what I'm talking about."

Billy set his beer on a nearby table, mumbled a string of off-color remarks, and stomped the short distance from his door to the cottage where Betty was now standing. His eyes scanned the empty rooms as he let out another string of four-letter words.

He turned, scratched his head, and looked to Betty for answers. She stared back with a blank gaze and shrugged her shoulders, remembering the two men who had come for donations. Had the movers left the door unlocked for thieves to stroll in later and clean the place out? Betty had left for work while they were putting books into large boxes and didn't sense any cause for alarm. She assumed they'd take the books and leave. Betty didn't volunteer any information.

Billy knocked on another tenant's door and got part of the mystery solved. A Goodwill truck had come late Saturday afternoon, the tenant said. Two men said they had a work order to remove all the furniture and appliances, adding he thought it was odd but seeing as they had a work order, he figured it was none of his business.

Billy stormed past the women and headed home. He grabbed the telephone and dialed 4-1-1. "Goodwill on Main Street," he barked into the telephone, repeating the numbers out loud. He clicked the receiver, then dialed the seven digits, not pausing to let his anger subside. He was determined to inflict pain on the hapless soul who answered his call.

Instead, he got a recording, a woman's voice telling him the store would be closed until further notice. He slammed the receiver on the cradle, repeated what he had heard, and yelled he'd take care of it "tomorrow."

Lauren snatched the receiver and dialed the same numbers, listened to the same recording, and banged the phone hard. Since Billy wasn't going to do anything, SHE would.

Charlee Bear came from behind and started licking Lauren's clenched fist. She dropped to her knees and threw her arms around her furry friend; he responded by nuzzling closer and whimpering. If dogs could talk, he was telling her everything would be okay. Maybe not now, but soon. His big brown eyes soothed Lauren.

"Did they take your bed too?" she said, stroking Charlee to calm his shaking. A moment later she realized it was her, not him, doing all the quivering. The anger and fear racing through her body gave way to a wave of calm. Charlee Bear magic, she thought.

"His bed's over at my house; it goes wherever he goes," Betty said. "It's like a favorite blanket to a toddler. Pick up his bed and he'll follow you anywhere. Got his food bowl too, and bag of food. The dog's got more than you got."

Lauren glared at Billy but knew it was useless to get him moving. He figured it was her problem if she wanted answers before tomorrow and told her so. She grabbed the phone book, pencil, and scrap paper, then scribbled down the address of Goodwill. Maybe they weren't answering their phone, but somebody was going to answer her questions. Today.

She asked Betty to take Charlee while she and Marissa headed downtown to retrieve the furnishings, including the oven and refrigerator. Nothing less would placate Lauren; she wanted the cottage furnishings loaded into a truck and returned by tonight.

She apologized to Marissa, feeling that she had let her friend down. But the sudden turn of events perked up the lawyer; finally, a simple problem with a simple solution.

No drama, no fuss, just a minor mix-up easily put right. Then, she smiled to herself, she could curl up with Charlee and face her own trauma drama.

Chapter 20

The two women walked to the newspaper's garage, found Lauren's gray VW beetle, climbed in, and headed north on Broadway. If they couldn't get the furniture returned by dusk, they agreed to get a hotel room for the night and catch up on some much-needed sleep.

The huge Goodwill logo sign loomed high above the one-story building, surrounded by an eight-foot metal fence. The entrance gate was bolted shut and laced with yellow crime scene tape; a squad car with flashing lights was parked in the middle of the street, flanked by officers waving gawkers back.

Lauren parked on a side street and sprinted to find answers for myriad questions racing inside her brain. Robbery? Homicide? Robbery was unlikely, not a lot of money collected at a donation center. She scanned the street looking for someone to give her some answers. She saw the *Journal's* crime reporter and headed his way to get details, only to be blocked by two burly men in uniforms.

She pulled out her press pass and demanded to be let through the police line. A car rounded the corner and caught their attention, the coroner's wagon. Lauren's face paled. "Body with bullets," she heard the officer tell the man behind the wheel. "Body's down in the shrubbery, been there least a day, maybe two or three."

Another dead body, something she expected in a big city but not so much in a sleepy beach township. Lauren would later look back at this moment as the calm before the storm. Decades of murder and deceit had set a tsunami in motion threatening to swallow her and the people she loved. There would be no early warning, no chance to head for safety, neither for her, her sister, nor the man she would give her heart.

The officers continued their conversation, but she heard only bits and pieces. Her subconscious was tying loose ends to separate all the turmoil like a pocket full of coins needing to be put in piles of pennies, nickels, and dimes.

She dismissed the idea of recovering her furniture, the mysterious ramblings of a sister who promised to reveal the details of their father-daughter talk, even thoughts of a man who had stirred her emotion the moment her eyes locked onto his. Tower something. At this moment she couldn't remember his last name any more than she could forget his eyes.

Lauren turned and headed for the car. She and Marissa would check in to the downtown hotel, get some dinner, and talk.

Chapter 21

Bill Stevens mindlessly shoved burnt toast into his mouth, gnawing as if it were shoe hide. A swig of coffee burned his mouth and forced him to spontaneously exhale, dotting the morning newspaper with brownish lumps.

The special agent propped his elbows on the table and rested his head in his massive palms, short fingers gently massaging his temples. The headache heading his way arrived early and was settling in for an extended stay. No aspirin was going to block the pain of the next few hours.

He cleaned up the mess, grabbed his briefcase, and headed for the downtown office, treating himself to a cab instead of the usual grueling morning ritual of hunting for an empty spot to park his sedan.

The idea, any idea, of what to say and how to phrase it bounced off the sides of his brain. Raw, painful pings that got him nowhere. He was going to have to walk a legal tightrope without a net. Too vague—the plan would yield unsatisfactory results and go nowhere. Too much information—he pictured some imaginary guy with scissors would gleefully clip the taut line. Stevens' reputation, his future, his everything depended on the conversation about to unfold.

The problem and its solution would have been easy if he was dealing with an ordinary agent. Not so much with Tower Stadler. How to proceed? How to win? His fingernails carved a path through his dark, wavy hair. His brow was puzzled; his lips sucked in while he pondered the next few hours.

Stadler was a brash, clever, 30-something special agent who always had an answer, usually the right answer. Stevens' career had soared over the past few years, ever since he hired the young agent and watched his team's investigative successes skyrocket. He was especially good at taking public bows for the team, but Stadler had made it clear he wasn't a team player. He wanted both the cases and the kudos. He wanted to play solo.

The last time the two were in the same room was a press conference a year ago and the only thing they exchanged were glares of contempt. One from self-righteousness, the other rage.

Now it was time to renegotiate their relationship. Stevens had no doubt that Stadler was the right man for the job; he worried that the younger agent would disagree.

Stadler was a big fish who didn't want to settle for a small pond. Stevens wished with all his heart that Stadler could be told the whole truth, but Gus Hagey had given him his marching orders, and there was nothing left to do but execute them. *Funny*, he thought. The word "execute" flashed in big red neon letters from the back of his brain to the front screen of his eyelids.

He settled behind the big desk temporarily assigned during operation "Logan's Run" and waited. The minute he saw Tower outside his office, the plan revealed itself in words and pictures. His shoulders relaxed; his hands unclenched.

He would tell the younger man only what he needed to get the job done. No letting on that he had been selected for this special assignment. The words he would use would make it all seem like a humdrum edict that required obedience sans objections. He was going to play the heavy.

"Boss," Stadler acknowledged, then plopped in a cushioned chair directly across from the man he despised. He offered a nod instead of his hand. The boss nodded in reply.

"No secret you don't want to be here any more than I want you here," Stevens said, leaning forward. His shoulders were drawn toward center; his clasped fists tightened. "None of this will take long if you do what you're told. No questions. Don't even furl your brows. Shake your head if you understand what I've asked of you."

Stadler nodded.

"We've got a problem with an overzealous agent who decided to color outside the law to get information," Stevens said. He was tempted to spill it all, but Stadler's nonchalant attitude had irked him. He was glad he had decided not to bring Stadler into the loop. The kid was causing himself unnecessary grief and some day he would pay dearly for his pride. Just not today.

"No need to get an apartment. We've made reservations for you at a downtown hotel in Santa Vista. What we need done shouldn't take more than a week."

Stadler wanted to speak but didn't. Clearly something had gone sour, very sour for his old boss to be forced to work with him again. He put his head on hold and decided to process the coming information via his gut. It's what made him so on target case after case. The brain could be fooled. People lied and sometimes even believed the lies that tripped from their lips. *But the gut, the gut always knows.*

"Your job is to retrieve a telephone bug from the office of Price Logan," Stevens said, without inflection. "Get in; get out." He tried to read Tower's thoughts, but his stone face wasn't offering any hint. His back remained straight, his face focused and unmoving.

"You are to report back to me with the device and the assurance that it was done without anyone knowing it was ever in the phone," the boss continued. "Then you are to forget we ever had this meeting. Understood?"

Stevens handed the young man a slip of paper with an unlisted phone number scribbled in pencil. "Get in; get out. Now, get out of here."

Tower stood up and turned his back on the man he loathed. He memorized the telephone number, crumpled the note, and tossed it over his shoulder, aiming for the desk. The boss was unaware of the smirk on Tower's face. The older man sighed, relieved the meeting was done.

The younger man inhaled the smell of blood in the water. The game was on and this time the victory would be his and his only.

Routine, that's how the assignment had been handed to him. But Tower knew there was nothing routine about this case. He had been collecting data on Price Logan over the years, eavesdropping while details of this investigation were discussed and filed away. Each time the Bureau came close, their whale slipped away. This was the department's Moby Dick that no one had been able to capture.

"Game on," Stadler said out loud, a challenge without consequences. Win or lose, the young FBI agent decided his last assignment would be one for the books.

Chapter 22

*H*unger trumped the need for sleep when the two women reached the hotel. Lauren headed to secure a room at the front desk while Marissa set out for the hotel's adjoining bar and grill. She asked for a table near the huge picture window and scooted across the padded bench until her body touched the cool glass. A waitress set down a glass of ice water and menu.

Marissa gazed out the window, then closed her eyes and took several deep breaths. She could feel her body relax. The afternoon was late, but still too early for the after-work bar crowd. A calmness washed over her body only to be interrupted by an unexpected rap on the window. She jumped, knocking over the water glass. One hand grabbed a fistful of napkins to block the liquid rushing toward her; the other acknowledged the man who caused the commotion.

There was an unexpected smile on her lips. She felt the warmth radiate, causing her cheeks to redden. Clearly, there was nothing subtle about the way she felt about this man.

She waved him inside, a move that astonished her usually reserved self. She heard a giggle and then laughed when she realized it came from her. By the time Tower Stadler reached the table, it was dry and reset with two water glasses. The waitress winked and offered a smile after checking out the tall, blond hunk.

"Good to see a friendly face," he said, motioning for the okay to sit down. Marissa waved her hand at the empty seat and offered a simple "Please join us."

Tower scanned the room for the other woman he had met on the plane, figuring that was the "us" Marissa referred. "Didn't expect to run into you so soon, but I was planning on calling to accept your offer for a picnic on the sand. Seattle rain has clouded my spirit, and I'm in need of good company and good wine under blue skies."

"Me too," Marissa said. "Chicago snow seems like it's been there forever, and I just got tired of being cold. I talked my sister into letting me crash in California for a short vacation. I need some quiet time to make plans, but it's been hectic and puzzling since we arrived."

Tower was about to ask a question when Lauren walked up to the table. Tower scooted over and patted the bench on his side of the table. "Sit," he said. "We were comparing our disappointing day. Mine couldn't have turned out worse if I'd walked through burning coal."

Lauren shot a glance at Marissa, wondering what she had told him about their current predicament. Marissa shook her head. Nothing, she had told him nothing.

The waitress came back with more water and menus. She asked if they wanted to order anything from the bar. It was the most agreeable thing any of them had been asked that day. Soon she brought a carafe of chardonnay and three chilled glasses. The wine was poured, a nonsensical toast was offered, and the three took deep sips before setting their glasses down.

"Well, guess we're all a little stressed," Lauren said. "It's all a puzzle. I can't understand why somebody called Goodwill to donate everything in the cottage. I mean, who donates a refrigerator and stove? Something isn't right about this. A lot of strange things have been happening since I first arrived at the newspaper."

Lauren then described her first encounter with the now deceased Harry Finnerty, the conflict over desks, his unbridled anger on the phone, and his dash to confront some man named Price Logan at his downtown office. She went into detail, putting words to the thoughts and observations tumbling inside her head.

"That car turned and came right at us at the last minute," Lauren said. "That was no accident. I witnessed a murder. I'd bet a substantial amount of cash that this Price Logan, whoever he is, is behind all this. Don't have the facts to support my feelings, but my gut is never wrong."

Tower put his wineglass to his mouth and took a swig at the mention of Logan's name. He needed time to come up with a strategy to get more information without appearing to have any reason to care. He offered a sympathetic nod and wondered why Lauren cared so deeply.

He wasn't the only one at the table who noticed her eyes fill with tears. Marissa offered an explanation: "Harry reminded Lauren of her grandfather who died when she was young. That's tough to get over when nobody will talk about how or why it happened."

"We were close," Lauren told Tower. "One day my grandfather stormed out of the house in a rage. Like Harry, he'd had too much to drink. Guess I was trying to protect Harry to redeem my guilt for not being there to help my grandfather. Crazy, mixed-up thinking, I know, but there you have it."

Tower desperately wanted details about her experience with Price Logan but dared not look too eager. Instead, he asked her about the moments before the accident.

Lauren recounted the confrontation with the secretary and the ensuing events that led to Harry being escorted out to the street by a couple of "thugs." Harry didn't get to see Price, but Lauren said she caught a glimpse of Logan's face just before the elevator doors shut. Logan heard the last of Harry's verbal tirade. "He's dead wrong, and you tell him Harry Finnerty said so."

Lauren decided it was time to change the subject. She turned her attention to Tower and asked what brought him to Santa Vista. He lied, offering only the promise of a job that might not materialize. He said he had a few days on his own and hadn't decided what to do with his time.

Lauren told him they were staying at the hotel while she tried to track down the whereabouts of her furnishings. "Couldn't get inside Goodwill to talk to anyone," she said. "The police shut the place down after they discovered a dead body near the parking lot. The cops said someone was shot and killed a few days ago. Strange... If I'm right, that makes two murders in as many days.

"And, no, I don't believe in coincidences."

Chapter 23

M arissa was quiet on the elevator ride to their tenth-floor room. A French dip sandwich and fries had sated her body's need for fuel, but now she craved a good night's rest to replenish the mental and emotional energy needed to process the secret her father had confessed. She and Lauren could talk tomorrow. Tonight, Marissa wanted to lay her head on a pillow and fall asleep thinking about the man seated across the dinner table. The thought made her smile.

"Want to tell me what that smirk on your face is all about, or shall I tell you," Lauren said, placing the room key into the lock. "It's been a long time since I've seen that dreamy look on your face."

"Let me have my thoughts all to myself, just for tonight," Marissa said. "We have a lot to talk about, but it's late and I'm tired. Please, tomorrow we'll talk."

"Agreed," Lauren said. "I want to soak in a hot tub and forget about today. Call the desk for a seven o'clock wakeup and we'll make our plans over breakfast. There's so much I want to get done, but I haven't a clue what comes first."

Sleep came reluctantly, eventually washing over both women until the sun peeked through the opened drapes. Marissa called first shot on a hot shower; Lauren rolled over, grunted, and started to think about what was ahead. She knew she had to discover more about Harry's time at the newspaper. Who had he offended enough to want him dead? She decided to check in with personnel and get a look at his work history. Then she would talk with his colleagues.

The two women entered the coffee shop just before eight and saw Tower sitting at a corner table. Lauren wanted coffee, a carafe, not a cup. "Make it black and strong," she told the waitress. She announced that she had a plan of action and needed to get to the newspaper early, no time for breakfast.

Lauren promised Marissa she would get an early lunch, offering a look that conveyed a verdict as final as the rap of a judge's gavel. No discussion. She sat silently, sipped then gulped the hot beverage. Several refills later, she pushed her chair back, grabbed her khaki jacket, and was gone.

Marissa read her friend's motive all wrong, assuming that Lauren was operating on the adage that "three's a crowd." She felt guilty and grateful, admitting to herself that she wanted her friend to disappear so she had Tower all to herself.

Infatuation swirled in Marissa's head, and electricity coursed through her body, shorting out the shared communication she and Lauren had depended on for the past decade. The ensuing days would prove this miscommunication both disastrous and deadly.

Tower was glad to be alone with Marissa, another misinterpretation courtesy of chemistry. He wanted to ask her about the last few days, not her day but rather Lauren's details of the encounter with Price Logan. Lauren might question his interest. Marissa, who was clearly infatuated with him, would think he was making small talk.

This wasn't the first time he'd taken advantage of the situation; it often worked to his ends.

"Your friend seems distracted and worried," Tower said, pausing to order bacon and eggs. Marissa told the waitress to bring oatmeal and whole wheat toast. "So, what's on Lauren's mind that makes her so distant?"

"She's decided that the reporter she replaced was murdered," Marissa said, "and too many things have been happening for it to be a coincidence. Neither of us believes in coincidences, never have. Life unfolds in a very orderly manner; the trick is not to second-guess but to deal with the facts and let them take you to a logical conclusion." Her words were punctuated with a long, hard chuckle.

"Lauren would be laughing at what I just said because I'm the dreamer. I was channeling Lauren. But seriously, it's important to keep an eye and a step ahead of her. When she gets it into her head that nothing is as it seems, Lauren won't stop until she finds what she's looking for. I'm the big picture; she's the detail person."

Marissa repeated all she knew about the death of Harry Finnerty: the confrontation at Price Logan's office and the walk home that ended in Harry's death. It was everything he already knew.

Then there was the emptied cottage, forcing the two women to check into the hotel. And, she told him about their trip to Goodwill to reclaim their furnishings, only to find the police investigating yet another death. This last one a homicide; no identification on the body.

They finished the last of their breakfast when, out of the blue, she asked him if he liked dogs. He smiled, and she got her answer and the direction for keeping his company for the next several hours.

They headed for the cottage to collect Charlee Bear for a walk along the beach. The morning clouds had disappeared, the waves were crashing along the shoreline, and the air smelled salty. Charlee wagged his tail as he led the two on a carefree trek a mile up the coastline. Shoeless, Marissa and Tower tackled the rushing waves, keeping the water at bay. Charlee rushed the water and jumped the waves, swimming with complete abandon.

Another golden retriever galloped toward Charlee, and the two wrestled in the sand before heading out for more swimming. A couple of kids ran toward the playful canines, shouting at their dog to come back.

The young girl looked up at Tower and Marissa and told them that Charlee and her puppy, Rose, were best friends. "Charlee and Rose hang out every day. Sometimes Charlee spends the whole afternoon at my house, but he always heads home when it starts to get dark," she informed them and told them her name was Elia.

The ten-year-old girl stared at the two oversized puppies and giggled. Her twin brother—"His name is Benj," Elia shared—headed up the coastline toting a fishing pole and can of sardines for bait. She told the adults that Benj never caught a fish but set out every day with the certainty that this was the day his luck would change.

"He wouldn't keep it anyway. Benj is too soft hearted. He wouldn't kill anything, not even a fly. Me either," Elia said, skipping off and calling her beloved Rose and Charlee Bear. The dogs looked up, stared at the cookies in her outstretched hand, and came running.

"Clever little girl," Marissa said. "Reminds me of me as a little girl."

Tower suddenly realized he had never known that measure of carefree abandon. He had always been guarded and stingy with his emotions. Just like his father, grins were rare. Giggles were reserved for special occasions when he was alone.

Any hope of finding out what made his father aloof and unhappy died when Tower buried him. The father never found peace and joy in life, never taught his son how to find it either.

Chapter 24

*L*auren drove to the newspaper with two goals—ask the editor for a couple days off to investigate Harry's death, then snoop in his personnel file to get a work history. She was sure it would lead her in the right direction, any direction. She was clueless but sure that Harry had been targeted.

The newly hired reporter tapped on the editor's door with a great deal of trepidation. She had no facts to back up her request for more time off, only a gut feeling that she was on to something big. Hugh Black waved Lauren inside and pointed to a chair across from his desk. He asked if she was ready to get to work. She answered with silence, still trying to form the words that would get her what she wanted.

"Yes and no," she finally uttered, scooting her chair closer to his desk. Her eyes pleaded for an open mind while she explained herself. "I want to spend a few days investigating Harry's murder, because that's what happened. Harry's death was no accident. I'm just certain of it. But I need time, I need to know more about the man to find out why someone wanted him dead."

"Nobody hated Harry more than he hated himself," Black said. "He didn't have a friend in the newsroom because he didn't want a friend. He came in three times a week to write and kept himself lubricated with vodka. Nobody liked the man, but nobody knew him well enough to hate him. Or want him dead, for that matter."

"You're wrong," Lauren told Black. "Give me a few days to prove it?"

Black chuckled at the sincerity of the reporter's determination. He had been told by her former editor to expect the unexpected. She came with high regard, so Black decided to give her the week, sure that she would find nothing but disappointment.

Lauren didn't tell Black about the altercation she witnessed at Price Logan's office. She didn't know if it had anything to do with the mystery she was investigating. But she was determined to find out. There was pure hate in Harry's eyes and voice when he threatened Price. But did the hate run both ways? And, more importantly, was whatever was going on serious enough to end in murder?

Lauren needed answers to myriad questions that hadn't even taken form in her subconscious; a puzzle with too many pieces lurked in the back of her mind. She had entered the mystery mid-plot, of that she was sure. What had happened in the past to create so much anger and hate? And how did the present add up to no future for a man she didn't really know? Who was Harry Finnerty? Good guy or bad guy? And why did she feel the need to know? What was all this to her?

If she had suspected any of what would unfold in the next week, perhaps she would have turned her back and walked away. Instead, Lauren charged full speed into the unknown.

The director of personnel was away for the week. His secretary had stepped away on a coffee break and the clerk was a temp. Getting a look at Harry's private information was turning out to be easier than she imagined. Lauren smiled at the girl sitting at the front desk and offered a lie, saying the editor sent her down to collect Harry Finnerty's work file.

The temp pointed to the metal cabinet where newsroom files were stored. She stood to lead the way, but a ringing phone captured her full attention. Lauren seized the moment and dared not look back to see if she was being watched. Blood rushed to her head and she knew her face was flushed. Lying never came easy to her.

Lauren opened the top drawer, fingers tripping over the alphabet until she reached the letter "F." "Falk," "Felson," then "Finnerty." She pulled the folder and placed it under her arm, walked to the door, nodded at the temp on the telephone, then headed to the elevator.

When the doors opened, Hugh Black emerged but was too busy talking with another reporter to notice Lauren. She felt her tense body relax when the editor rushed by without noticing her. She knew she had crossed a line; he didn't suspect the young reporter could be devious. Not that she was going to turn around and make things right. Not on your life. Not on Harry's life.

Lauren grabbed the car keys from her jacket pocket and pulled out a yellowed photo along with the keys. She remembered finding it in Harry's dog training book on the plane to Seattle but paid it no attention. She stuffed the photo into Harry's folder and tossed it on the passenger seat. The photo stayed up; a stamped envelope escaped from a loose paper clip, then floated to the floor and under the seat. She never noticed.

Lauren headed for the hotel, sure that information in the folder would offer her the pieces of a puzzle she was determined to solve. Once assembled, the picture would reveal his murderer. She opened the hotel door, placed the "Do Not Disturb" on the outside, then double locked the door with a bolt and chain for extra security.

She smoothed the blanket on the unmade bed and then opened the folder and placed the contents in piles from past to present. She wasn't surprised to find disciplinarian notes attached to angry letters from readers protesting his treatment of them. Threats, but no lawsuits were ever filed.

There was an assortment of drunk and disorderly tickets and court appearances. He'd had his driver's license revoked after a series of warnings a decade ago. She counted four suspensions from Hugh Black for journalistic misconduct. Clearly, Harry had offended a lot of people.

She picked up the lone snapshot, glanced at the two young men in the photo. Her jaw dropped. She was staring at the face of Tower Stadler linked arm-in-arm with another man the same age. Both wore lettermen's jackets and were leaning on a dark sedan with a DeSoto logo.

It looked surreal—the old and the new clashed and made no sense. She put the photo back into the file and kept searching for more clues.

There was no next of kin; Harry was an only child and his parents had died decades ago. There was no person listed as a contact in case of emergency; instead, the newspaper's general telephone number was penciled in. Lauren wondered, how could anyone be so unloved but not hated? More and more, it seemed his dog's devotion was the only source of warmth and acceptance Harry had ever received.

Still, Lauren felt a need for retribution for a life lost. If not for Harry, then for his beloved Charlee Bear. She was more determined than ever to put a name and a face to the person who thought he had gotten away with murder.

Chapter 25

On the same day Harry Finnerty was mowed down by a black sedan, ex-con Earl Watson walked into the Chicago law offices of Kromer, Somme and Thornton. He hadn't been there long enough to shake the icy chill from his bones when he was met with an even chillier reception.

The only words he uttered were a request to see attorney Ben Taylor. The young receptionist explained that there was no Ben Taylor at the firm, but there was a Marissa Taylor. She was cut off midsentence; the boss ushered the intruder out the door and into the elevator.

Not to be discouraged, Watson bought a newspaper and settled in the building's first-floor lobby to wait for the receptionist to get off work. He knew she would be willing, even eager, to see him again. Before he could turn to the sports section, he heard the distinctive click of high heels on the marble floor, fast and furious. He recognized the young woman and watched as she headed for the exit. She slung her coat over one shoulder and rebalanced a heavy cloth tote bag with the other hand.

She blew past him without a glance. The woman was halfway out the door when the tote snagged a metal knob, pulling her backwards and off balance. She regained her balance before she fell to the floor, spitting a string of invectives that made the ex-con blush.

Watson watched her pass through the glass doors, then decided to follow a safe distance behind to wait for an opportune moment to engage her in conversation. She headed for a nearby bus bench, sat, and switched out her heels for rubber-soled flats. He was prepared to board a bus and take a seat next to her but she got up and headed across the street.

Snow flurries blurred the blue neon sign flashing in a huge window across the four-lane avenue. She walked to the curb, waited for the light to change, and headed for the door of a cocktail lounge. Watson folded his coat collar up over his cheeks, both for cover from a sudden icy wind but also to hide his face, then followed her lead.

Watson raced across four lanes, opened the bar door, and adjusted his eyes to the darkness. He took a seat at the horseshoe-shaped bar, directly across from the woman. When she looked his way, he smiled and waved her over to the empty seat on his left. Her spirits were suddenly lifted; a flirty smile crossed her lips. She collected her purse and tote and edged her way around the bar.

"Fancy bumping into you here," she said. "I'm Julie."

"Hi Julie, I'm Earl." He found his reaction equal parts awkward and shy. Too many years had passed since he had struck up a casual conversation with a female; he searched for words. Julie found it charming. She had expected him to be cocky and too sure of himself. She was rarely the target of attention from a good-looking man; instead, she used her gregarious personality to attract attention.

Julie kept her voice steady and disinterested, lest he think she was too eager. Not that she wasn't anxious to take this accidental meeting from bar to bed; her body was hungry for his. She fancied herself a liberated woman and allowed her sexuality to have its way without guilt. After all, the new decade promised more sexual freedom for young women. She felt drunk with the idea.

Earl listened as she talked about herself, pausing occasionally to ask him a question. He was good at being vague and reflecting the conversation away from himself. Again, Julie found this charming. He bided his time, asking her about her career goals. Did she fancy a law career? Was that why she worked at the law firm? Did she like the work? Was she well compensated?

Julie stopped talking and a puzzled look came over her face. She'd never thought about going to law school, never really thought much about careers. She took the job to meet eligible attorneys, find one with money, get married, and be free of financial worries. Not that she said any of this out loud.

"Yeah, I was thinking about law school after college," she lied. "But, I'm beginning to realize just how boring the law can be—too much research and paperwork. Not interesting and fast-paced like on TV shows. That's why I quit today."

Earl was a seasoned liar and could spot another liar a mile down the road, like the one sitting on the barstool to his left. His interest was piqued. She didn't quit them, the boss quit her. But why? What had just happened?

"I didn't get you in any trouble with my questions, did I? Because I would feel really bad if I did," he said.

Before she answered, Julie weighed her response, wondering if having him feel bad could work to her advantage. "Well, kinda," she said. "They weren't all that happy with my work, but the boss really screamed at me when you left. He wanted me to repeat everything I told you. He was furious with both me and you. I told him, well, word for word what I told you. He slammed the door to his office, made a phone call, and then came back and handed me an envelope with cash. Said not to come back."

"But you really didn't tell me anything," Earl said. "He told me Ben Taylor moved to Boston decades ago, so I can't see why he got so hot under the collar."

"That's just it," Julie said. "Ben Taylor moved to Seattle, not Boston. I know because his daughter works at the firm. When she was introduced to me, some of the men made a big deal about her being Ben Taylor's daughter. She would have been there today except she took off for a long weekend to see her parents and sister, Lauren. And I was the one who made her plane reservations for Seattle."

Watson excused himself, said he was headed for the men's room, and told Julie to order herself another drink. He smiled at her, squeezed her shoulder, and mentioned something about dinner.

Earl Watson left through the back door and never looked back. He needed money for a plane ticket to Seattle, new clothes, and a place to plan his next move.

The crowds along the avenue were thick and hectic. People were coming and going; some racing to get home from work while others headed into the city for Christmas shopping. The crowds were so frenetic that every step forward, his body was knocked sideways. Then he smiled. The frenzy was the answer to his poverty.

As a teen, he had perfected the art of picking pockets. Amid the commotion, Watson felt giddy, as if he had walked into an unguarded bank vault. His mouth twisted into a holiday grin, and his fingers itched to see if he still had the touch.

He did. Less than an hour later, Earl Watson figured he had lifted enough wallets to shop for new clothes and find a hotel room to catch up on his sleep. Tomorrow he would head to O'Hare and catch a plane for the West Coast. He had a stack of twenty-dollar bills, some tens and fives and seven credit cards. A driver's license showed that one man even looked enough like him to be his brother.

Watson thought about ditching the plastic but decided to pocket one and toss the rest. He kept the brown leather wallet, stuffing the cash, credit card, and ID into separate slots.

Watson headed for Macy's and found a willing clerk to bring him everything he requested, from shoes and socks to shirts and shorts. She brought him a leather jacket, said it looked like it was made for him.

An hour later, he followed her to the cashier station, pulled out his wallet, and paused when she asked how he would be paying today. "Cash or credit?" she asked. He pulled out the plastic, handed it to the clerk, smiled and winked.

"Let's go ahead and put it on my card," he said. She thanked him. Earl Watson mentally thanked Jules Corder, the man who looked enough like him to be his brother. He signed the receipt and she handed him his packages, telling him to be sure and come back again real soon.

He wanted a beer but headed for a diner and settled for hot coffee laced with teaspoons of sugar. He ordered a burger and fries, inhaled his food, then hit the streets in search of a canvas bag to stash his new duds.

Next came some well-deserved sleep before he faced his first Saturday morning with no one telling him when to rise or what to eat. He checked into a small hotel, stripped off his cheap suit, and stood under a hot stream of water until the shower pipes clanged and the water chilled. He dried off and slipped under the sheets buck naked. Sleep came swiftly and sunrise followed too soon.

Chapter 26

On a Saturday morning in early December 1979, Earl Watson opened his eyes and stared up at a small window draped with cheap linen. A smile crossed his lips. He was thinking about Marie.

He blinked twice and snickered at the sight of the Chicago sky sans steel bars. He pinched himself, just for laughs, then walked to the door to make sure he could walk out. First mornings on the "outside" world can be startling, he'd been told. Yep, even a little scary. But the thought of finding Marie calmed him. He was on a mission and his next stop would be Seattle. He prayed that he could make his daughter understand.

On that same Saturday, some 2,000-plus miles west, the daughter he longed to see was learning about him for the first time. Ben Taylor decided to reveal secrets he had guarded for decades. He told her about her biological father and how she came to be Marissa Taylor.

He knew he was going against his wife's wishes, and the decision hadn't been made lightly. He knew, too, that Marissa had every right to know, especially since he had learned Earl Watson had been released from prison and was on a quest to find his daughter, Marie.

That same Seattle sky that darkened the talk between Ben and Marissa rained down on Lauren Foster. Her thoughts were anchored in yesterday. The image of Charlee Bear with his chin on Harry's lifeless chest popped into her head; the big dog's guttural moans filled her ears.

Lauren flicked a lone tear that escaped from the corner of her eye and wiped her cheek dry with her sleeve. This thing about feeling emotions was overrated. She did what came naturally, and that was nothing. Think about something else and soldier on, she told herself.

A couple of miles away that same Saturday, Tower Stadler nursed a banging hangover—one of only a handful he had experienced in his lifetime. People drank to forget, but Tower had no intention of either forgetting or forgiving the people who were trying to kill his dream.

Terse and vague, the letter delivered the day before had sent him into a tailspin. He would pack a suitcase and show up in San Francisco in two days. He could swallow his pride, but there would be no keeping it down. Tower would take one last assignment for the Bureau, then quit. And he was going to do it his way.

South in Santa Vista, California, business tycoon and philanthropist Price Logan cursed the daylight that same Saturday morning and kicked at a tall pile of rubbish. The stolen furnishings from Harry Finnerty's ocean cottage had yielded no secrets. He had taken apart every piece of furniture and appliances, looking for the film. Nothing.

Price had never hated Harry Finnerty more than at this moment. His only wish was that he could kill the blackmailer twice. This second time would be slow and painful. Damn.

Earl, Marissa, Lauren, Tower, and Price. All facing unsettling uncertainties and painful emotions. In less than a week, the five would cross paths in the picturesque community of Santa Vista.

One of them would die.

Chapter 27

Earl Watson dressed in khaki pants, sweater, and boots. He grabbed his new leather jacket and headed for the same Chicago eatery where he had downed burger and fries the night before. The fifties diner was comfortable, near the hotel, and the food was good. The waitress brought his order of coffee, eggs scrambled hard, and crispy bacon. He chomped on white toast slathered with real butter and strawberry jam.

He was remembering how much he liked the taste of food cooked to order. Breakfast in the joint was usually raw and runny. The bread was cold and chewy. He looked around the diner and thought the rest of the crowd couldn't know how blessed they were to be in a warm room with hot food.

The ex-con finished his bacon and eggs and sipped the last of his coffee. He realized his stomach ached, not so much from gulping his breakfast but rather from guilt gnawing at his belly. It had taken him less than 24 hours to break every "swear to God" vow he had made over the past two decades. He promised to live a clean life, to make amends for all the damage he had done. There was no way to undo a killing other than to lead a good life, or what was left of it. He needed his daughter's understanding and forgiveness. He wanted a second chance to be in her life.

Watson had to face the financial damage to the hundreds who fell victim to his street theft. He had taken thousands of dollars from strangers and lived and gambled with their hard-earned money. He wondered how to repair that one but figured he would face that issue after he found his daughter.

In his mind, he swore he had meant every promise, but his current actions proved him a liar. And liars don't stay sober. So that was it, he was gambling with his sobriety, and his body was reacting unconsciously to that realization. A shiver ran up and down his spine. The consequences of his actions were predictable; many ex-cons recounted stories of going off the rails soon after their release. Freedom has its own rules.

He turned the problem over in his mind and reasoned those earlier vows were easy to make because he never expected to be tested. He was dealt a "life sentence" and thought he would die behind bars. This sudden freedom frightened him. He was beginning to believe a drink would steady his nerves and straighten his thinking.

Watson understood that each man was only as good as his word. He had spent much of his free time in the prison library catching up on the education he had once valued so little. His favorite subjects were psychology and philosophy. The words on those books came to life, and with that realization, Watson paid his bill and headed for a nearby phone booth. He grabbed the directory hanging from a metal chain and searched the alphabet with the single-mindedness of a drowning man reaching for a lifejacket. When the voice answered, "Alcoholics Anonymous," Earl Watson reached out for help.

A short conversation later, a man was dispatched to pick up Watson and get him to a meeting. He stayed for the morning meeting and felt better. Several afternoon meetings later, Watson felt strong and ready to resume his mission to find his daughter.

First, he needed to make a list of the names and addresses of the people whose wallets he had stolen. He would start making amends once he found a job and cashed a paycheck. Meanwhile, it was back to Plan A: Find Ben Taylor so he could help him find Marie.

Watson located a small travel agency and bought a one-way ticket to Seattle with his "borrowed" plastic. He figured he had another 24 hours before the man's card number would appear on the "stolen" list. Mentally, he added the cost of the flight ticket to the Macy's bill. He would have to work months to pay back Jules Corder. But he would, he said to himself. And he meant it.

He asked the travel agent if she could look up the phone number for an attorney by the name of Ben Taylor in Seattle. Watson said he was an old classmate and he was flying out to surprise him. The agent telephoned a Seattle operator and got the number, then covered the mouthpiece with her hand to ask if he needed an address too. He nodded and watched as her right hand scribbled the name, address, and phone number of his former attorney.

Watson congratulated himself on finding the lawyer who could point him in the right direction in his search for Marie. What Earl Watson never imagined was that he would be talking to Marie's adopted father as well as his long-ago pro bono attorney. He would find out soon enough.

The travel agent thanked Mr. Corder for his business, caressed his hand as she returned his credit card, then made him promise he would return when he got back to town. He flirted; she beamed. And they never saw one another again.

On the way back to the hotel, Watson ducked into a pizzeria for a couple of sausage slices and washed them down with iced tea. He stared at the folder the travel agent had handed him and felt very satisfied. His stomach was as content as his conscience.

He would be flying out Sunday evening and knocking on Ben Taylor's door sometime Monday morning. He would need a day to plan a conversation that would entice the attorney to help him in his search. Adoption records were private and he had no hope on his own to gain access to the file. He knew Mr. Taylor had a daughter and that the unconditional love he felt for her would persuade him to help him find Marie.

She would be 25 years old now, probably had a husband and children. Earl laughed at the idea of being a grandfather. Time had been suspended while he was in prison. He felt like a 20-something out to explore and exploit the world. Just not tonight; his head seemed as heavy as his heart felt light. Funny thing about closing in on a heart's desire. It made you unsure if the reality would be as good as the dream.

He slept well that night and ate more bacon and eggs, toast and jam in the morning. Then Earl decided to find one last AA meeting, and this time he would speak.

"My name is Earl and I have been sober for twenty-three years," he told the group. When the crowd offered him a well-deserved ovation, Watson held his hands up to quash the applause. "I did it the easy way. I was in prison," he confessed. "No booze there. So technically, I've been sober for only a couple of days out in the real world. I worked the program inside and thought I'd be safe outside the walls. But, you know, I didn't last twenty-four hours without seeking out you guys. Dealing with reality without a buzz is going to be hard. These streets are really different from the last time I walked them."

Earl stayed after the meeting, drank coffee, and talked with a couple of guys before leaving for the airport. His late afternoon flight would arrive in time for him to eat dinner, find a hotel, and get a good rest before setting out for his former attorney's home.

Chapter 28

Earl Watson's first plane ride was uneventful if you could call being suspended in the air for several hours commonplace. He had seen and heard planes circling near the prison but never thought he would be inside one. But here he was, eating a roast beef sandwich and corn chips thousands of feet in the air.

The plane landed with a jar and the ex-con waited to release his seat belt until the engines quieted; he was the last one to leave the cabin. Watson collected his leather bag and headed down the metal stairway attached to the plane. He had swapped blue skies for gray ones, snow for rain. He felt a mixture of joy and trepidation. A new life was out there waiting to be discovered. He shivered.

Watson rented a room at a motel near the airport and meant to take a shower, then get some sleep. He lay down to catch his breath and woke up six hours later. The anxiety of air travel had exhausted him to the bones. He found a coffeepot on the dresser and decided to brew a cup and then find some food to quiet his stomach. He wasn't particularly hungry; his mind was consumed by thoughts of Marie.

He found a couple of candy bars and peanuts in his bag, enough to hold him till breakfast. He stirred the coffee with his chocolate bar, following a futile search for either sugar or a spoon. He was used to not having choices; it made life easier, he thought. He could always make do, no matter what came his way. Some called it lazy, he called it survival.

The ex-con stripped naked and crawled between heavily starched sheets and closed his eyes. Sleep eluded him. When the sun rose, so did he. First thing, breakfast. His mouth watered for bacon and hot cakes swimming in butter and syrup. He didn't order coffee, more room for food, he reasoned. Besides, his nerves were already at full attention, and the last thing he needed was caffeine.

He got out a map of the city and traced the path from the airport to the Taylors' house with his index finger. It would be ten o'clock before he could get there, plenty late enough to seem casual. Watson headed back to the airport, where he had seen a car rental agency.

"Sorry, Jules," he murmured. "I promise to add it to the tab."

The nondescript blue sedan seemed easy enough to drive; a couple of times around the back lot and he had it mastered. Traffic was light, and he set out on the main roads with the folded map at his side. Watson made a couple of wrong turns, mainly because he hadn't mastered the art of merging in the rain. The windshield wipers worked at a fast pace. He kept the radio turned off, no distractions. A warm rush of air pushed through vents near his feet. It felt good, this new world. He could get used to it.

Watson found the Taylor house but decided to circle the block a couple of times to see if anyone came or went. Eventually, he pulled into an open space across from the two-story mansion, put the car in park, and turned off the engine. He steadied his breathing and rehearsed his lines a couple of times before approaching the front door.

Less than a minute after he rang the doorbell, an older woman appeared. He smiled, tipped his hat, and said he hoped he had found the right address. The woman laughed. "Depends. Who're you looking to find?"

Watson was about to answer when the rain came pouring down. "Come out of the wet," she admonished. "We can talk inside."

"I'm in town for meetings and I remembered that my college fraternity brother lives in Seattle," he said. "Looking for Ben, Ben Taylor. I wanted to surprise him."

"Oh, I'm sorry to disappoint you, sir," the woman said, adding that her name was Evelyn and that she worked for the family, "and have for a lot of years."

"Is Ben out for just a short time? I could come back," Watson offered, introducing himself as Jules Corder.

"Oh dear, Ben is out of town on business for a couple of days. Joan will be home after five o'clock," Evelyn said. "Would you like to leave a note?"

"Sure," he said, looking as disappointed as he felt. Evelyn led him into Ben's office, pointed to the desk, adding, "You'll find stationery and a pen." He took off his wet jacket, folding it inside out to keep the water from soaking the rug. He looked at Ben's neat desk: blotter, pens, paper, and a cluster of family photos.

He was about to ask her another question, but his mouth turned dry, his voice cracked, and a cough threatened to close off his airway. Evelyn rushed to his side, swatted his back with an open palm, and told him to hold on while she ran to get him water.

Tears filled his eyes. His face turned red, then ashen. Evelyn wanted to call an ambulance, but Watson insisted he was fine, just needed a minute. "You ever swallow the wrong way?" he asked. "That's what I get for trying to talk and swallow at the same time."

He explained that he was just excited about connecting with his old friend, told her he knew Ben had done well, better than most in his old fraternity. His hand reached for a family portrait, said he figured Ben would marry his college sweetheart. "And these are his kids? Two girls?" he asked.

"Well, yes and no," Evelyn said. "That's their daughter Marissa standing next to Joan; the one standing next to Ben is their adopted daughter, Lauren Foster. Both girls are smart and pretty. Lauren is a reporter at a newspaper in Santa Vista in California. Both girls left for there on a plane this morning. I helped raise Marissa from the time she was a toddler. Guess I'm going on and on, but I do love those girls."

"I would expect nothing but beauty and brilliance from Ben's children." Watson smiled. "Marissa is wearing the red sweater, right? Lauren is in white? You've known the family for a lot of years, since both were just kids?"

"No, the two girls met in college. Ben and Joan adopted Lauren informally, you know. Her parents died when she was young. Her aunt raised her, but she passed when Lauren was a freshman in college. She had no one really, only us, and Lauren was born to be family."

Evelyn offered Jules coffee or tea. He declined and said he'd write a short note to Ben and be on his way. She left the den to clean the living room; minutes later he walked out of the office. In a smooth movement, Earl Watson, aka Jules Corder, clasped Evelyn's hands between his, squeezed gently, and let go.

He thanked her for her kindness, handed her the envelope with the note to Ben folded inside, and walked out into the cool rain pelting his warm face.

Earl Watson reached into his jacket pocket and pulled out the folded picture of Marie, faded and worn from ten years of handling. It was the same face as the one in a gold frame on Ben's desk; his Marie, taken on her 16th birthday. The seemingly altruistic attorney had stolen his daughter, made her his. Ben had given her a good life, yes, but at what cost? Did the ex-con get fair representation at his trial? Or had Ben Taylor made sure he got life in prison so he could steal Marie and make her his daughter? And why did he send the photo? It had to be Ben who sent it. Did he send it to taunt Earl?

Too many questions with answers buried in the past and no one there to answer him. Earl's mood went from sad to mad and spiraled into vengeance.

He intended to fuel his ire with high-octane alcohol. Sobriety be damned; he was going to get stinking drunk and then find his daughter in Santa Vista. He was her father, not Ben. He should get all Marie's love; Ben deserved none. Ben was her past. He was going to claim what was rightfully his.

Chapter 29

Somewhere between the Taylor house on Beacon Hill and downtown Seattle, Watson's temper cooled. His anger turned inward, and he no longer wanted to block his pain with booze. Revenge tasted sweeter.

Self-talk and rationalizations ate at his earlier resolve; he knew he was his own worst enemy. Perhaps, he thought, it was more than just alcohol that fueled his lousy life. What did he hear one guy call it at an AA meeting? "Stinkin thinkin"?

"Guilty," he said out loud. "Now what am I going to do about it?"

Watson laughed, cried, and cursed on his downtown drive in search of an AA meeting. He wanted to stay angry and go on a rant, but reason ruled instinct. He found help and understanding on the other end of the AA phone line for the second time in as many days.

A half hour later, he was seated in the back row at a community hall. There were dozens of noon meetings to help alcoholics, every day in every town all over the country. He knew he could find others like himself, fighting the same demons.

He didn't want to talk; Watson needed to listen to sober people who once thought like he was thinking now. He needed a sober person to speak words to help him recalibrate his emotions and get him back on the right track. Anger wasn't going to get him where he wanted to go; seemed he always picked anger as the "go to" solution for any problem.

"Enough," he said out loud, to no one in particular. A couple of men two rows up turned to look his way; the older man quietly made his way to the back of the room and plopped down in the chair next to Watson.

When the meeting ended, the man introduced himself as Jerry, reached into his jacket pocket, and took out a token. "I've been in AA for five years," he said. "The fellow who gave me this said I would know when to pass it on. I've carried it with me during my sobriety and it has served me well."

He put the metal token into Watson's palm, then closed Earl's fingers shut. "When you leave here and put your ass on a barstool, take this out and ask yourself one question. 'Am I willing to pay the price for the choice I am about to make?' Think hard, then put this back in your pocket and get the hell out of there."

Watson stared at the man's face, and asked Jerry, "What difference can a token make?" The stranger didn't speak, just smiled and walked away. The ex-con turned the metal piece over in his right hand and saw that it was a 25-year sobriety token. He thought about what Jerry said and wondered, given a choice, with time enough to process the consequences, would booze lose its hold on him? People who worked the program understood that drinking was a one-way ticket back to hell; it took time and trouble to learn, some never did. Watson's eyes scanned the crowd, but Jerry had disappeared.

The man had saved him from himself today, but he would never see Jerry again to thank him. He put the token in his pant pocket and made the decision to head for Santa Vista.

Watson was feeling grateful. Grateful to Jerry, grateful to the voice on the phone who had directed him to this meeting, and grateful to his higher power. Funny, he thought, someone or something was saving him from himself. If he believed in a God, he would thank Him too. But no loving God would have allowed him to be born into the suffering he had endured, both as an infant and later as an inmate.

Earl Watson was sure of very few things, but he was sure there was no God. His higher power, he determined, was his daughter Marie, and the need to make amends to her served as his driving force. And it was working to his advantage.

He found a filling station, filled the gas tank, and bought a map to point the way south from Seattle to San Francisco. It was a straight shot south, just over 800 miles on Interstate 5. On his way out of town, Watson pulled into the drive-thru lane at a fast-food chain restaurant. He rolled down his window and yelled into a clown's face, ordering burgers, fries, and a cola with enough caffeine to fuel him for the long drive.

Watson had decided to leave the blue sedan rental car in San Francisco and switch to another identity for the next rental car, a gray sedan. Jules Corder had served his purpose and it was time for him to retire without a trace. Watson had several wads of cash in his leather bag, enough to keep him going during the next leg of his journey. Anyway, if funds ran low, Watson figured he could always drive back to San Francisco to refill his coffers. He really didn't have a plan once he got to Santa Vista, thought it would be wise to keep a low profile and see how things unfolded.

His first stop would be the town's newspaper to find Lauren Foster's address. Then he would get some food, find lodging, and get some much-needed sleep. And he wanted to walk on the beach barefoot with wet sand oozing between his toes. He had never seen an ocean; the idea made him hum out loud.

Chapter 30

*A*fter his beach jaunt with Marissa, Tower returned to his hotel room. His uniform, embroidered with the name "Burt," arrived freshly starched and pressed. The time had come to deliver on his sole task—debugging an office telephone, namely Price Logan's private phone. At least his FBI boss thought that was all he was up to, but Tower had other ideas.

He showered, shaved, and donned the telephone company's uniform. "Burt" checked himself in the mirror and decided that no blue collar worth a damn ever looked and smelled this fresh. He needed to get real. Tower set about making it look like he'd had a long, hard shift and was in no mood to be denied access to the last job that stood between him and a brew at a nearby tavern.

The company van had been delivered outside his hotel, courtesy of his boss, FBI agent Bill Stevens. It was getting to be late afternoon, and secretaries were anxious to cover their typewriters and get home. Time to make his move.

He picked up the phone, dialed Logan Enterprises, and asked to speak to Price Logan. He was transferred to the president's private secretary, who said that Mr. Price would be out of the office for the rest of the afternoon. She politely asked what this was regarding, but static filled the airway; then the phone went dead.

Tower dialed Stevens' private line and spoke two words: green light. Then he slammed the phone on the cradle for punctuation. Didn't do any good, just felt good.

As the telephone truck pulled away from the curb with Tower behind the wheel, Lauren was pulling up. She yelled his name and waved to get his attention, determined to get answers to her photo mystery. He didn't see her.

Since this conversation would be delayed, Lauren decided to use the time to schedule an interview with Price Logan. She turned back to the parking garage, sat in her car, and pulled out her reporter's notebook to jot down a few questions before heading out.

On the drive over to Price's downtown office, Lauren wondered why Tower had signed on with the telephone company. He said he was looking for work, but she imagined Tower with an intellectual and glamorous job, something more challenging as a career choice.

And how had he secured this job so fast? Goes to show, she thought, one more item to add to the things-are-not-as-they-seem basket.

Then her thoughts turned to Price. How could she get him to talk to her? What would be the hook? The answer came as quickly as the questions. She would need the details of his life if she was assigned to write an "advanced obituary." Both flattering and disconcerting, the rich and powerful had their life stories ready for print in case the unexpected happened.

Price Logan was rich and powerful; it was a natural entry for snooping into his life successes and failures. She was determined to find out how and where the lives of Harry Finnerty and Price Logan had intersected. Her gut told her it was vital, and her brain concocted a logical plan. That's the way she worked best—her brain took orders from her gut. Her heart shut them both down when emotions ran hot.

Lauren parked her car near the building's entrance. She crossed the cavernous lobby, headed for the express elevator to Logan's headquarters. The doors yawned open, and she stepped in and rehearsed her opening line to gain both entry into his office and his life story. No reason for suspicion. She was a new reporter in town on one of her first assignments, and the two had never met.

When the elevator reached the top floor, Logan's secretary looked up from her typewriter and greeted Lauren with a concerned expression. She told Lauren how sorry she was to hear about the death of her colleague, Harry Finnerty. Lauren reached for a business card, smiling as she tried to distance herself from that first meeting.

"Thanks, but we had just met hours earlier," Lauren said. "I followed him here to try to convince him that I had nothing to do with his reassignment to the copy desk. He was drunk, you know, he drank a lot. I was there when he stepped in front of the car and got hit. I feel sorry for the driver. He needs to know Harry was the one at fault. He just stepped in front of the car..."

Lauren knew she was talking too much. She hadn't counted on someone remembering her face. She took a deep breath. "I'd never seen a person die before... Guess it kind of rattled me."

The older woman nodded and accepted the business card Lauren offered.

"My first assignments are meant to get me familiar with the most influential leaders in the community," Lauren continued. "No surprise that your boss is on the top ten list. As gruesome as it sounds, we have a file of biographies that need to be updated in case of death. I know it's off-putting but it's tough to get an important person's accomplishments accurate and complete on deadline. Too much can be overlooked or gotten wrong."

The older woman nodded and told her she would talk with Mr. Logan to see if he wanted to arrange for an interview. She started to speak again when the door to the private office clicked open. The secretary turned to the telephone repairman and asked if he had fixed the problem. Static on the line had caused problems all morning. She was pleased to have the glitch fixed while the boss was out of the office.

The repairman touched his hat and let out a very southern "Yes ma'am. Short on the mainframe, nothing serious." One look at his face made Lauren turn away, knocking over her purse. She scrambled to collect her comb, compact, and writing tablet, then stalled, pretending to search for her car keys.

Tower hurried to help the lady in distress, stepping on her left foot as he came too close. She let out a loud yelp; the repairman apologized profusely with a string of very sincere and repentant "sorry, ma'ams." His apologies silenced any attempt by Lauren to speak his name or ask questions. She realized he had aimed for her foot. She put on her best poker face while she rubbed her bruised toes.

When the elevator doors opened and swallowed him, the secretary commented on how handsome and polite the repairman was. "Good to see a young man with old-fashioned manners. If I were thirty years younger, I would have flirted with Burt." No poker face here; she was remembering a time when she was young and desirable. Time had stolen both and she was wise enough to leave young love to the young. She shook her head, returning to the present, promising to talk with Mr. Logan and get back to Lauren soon.

"Thank you. I'm new at the paper and anxious to make a good impression on my editor. Tell your boss I won't take more than an hour of his time."

She heard chatter coming from a long hallway on the left and spotted the two men who had escorted Harry out of the building just days ago. It was clearly time for her to make her exit the way she entered. She feigned a sneeze to cover her face with her hand, then made her escape unnoticed.

Chapter 31

*L*auren raced back to the hotel to confront Tower Stadler, who wasn't the out-of-work nomad he pretended on their plane ride from Seattle to San Francisco. Of that, she was sure. Good Guy or Bad Guy, she needed to know.

Her inner compass accurately judged people, and she had confidence in her ability to assess people—both their intent and content. She wanted to know more about Mr. Tall, Blonde, and Handsome before either encouraging or warning her sister. Clearly, Marissa was smitten.

Lauren liked Tower well enough but thought him too smooth and accustomed to getting his way with the ladies. Even the older secretary had a faraway look when she commented, "If only I were younger." She was old enough to know better and not fall victim to a Casanova. Marissa, not so much. Her sister believed in the innate goodness of every human being. Circumstances and bad luck made a few souls falsehearted and deceitful, Marissa begrudgingly allowed.

Lauren had been the beneficiary of Marissa's complete love and trust. She assumed the role of protector from the start of their friendship. There was something fragile, even childlike when you stared into Marissa's eyes. Until recently, Lauren thought her sister had lived a fairy-tale life—stable, loving parents, continuity, and life pretty much without a bump or spill.

When Ben and Joan revealed Marissa's adoption, Lauren figured it would make Marissa feel more wanted and cherished. The childless couple had gone looking for her; no accident here.

Lauren, on the other hand, knew her arrival was an unwelcome surprise and served to interrupt her parents' carefree lifestyle. Not that she was unloved; first Papa, then Aunt Sarah. After their deaths, Ben and Joan asked her to join the family and thereafter spoke of two daughters, not one.

In the long night that loomed, the young journalist was to learn the details of her sister's adoption. Namely, good had been born of evil.

Marissa waited for Lauren to return to the hotel room lying on the bed in a fetal position and weeping into a pillow. Inconsolable and frightened, she needed her sister to help her make sense of it all. Pictures of a child hovering in the corner, hiding behind a blanket played in her subconscious. They were real enough for Marissa to pluck the figures from fantasy to reality.

The unnamed fear that filled her body was relentless. Was she reliving a memory recounted by one of her young clients? How could someone else's nightmares loom so real, even smell and taste so real?

Her teeth pinched at her bottom lip, spilling a trickle of blood down her chin. She remembered blood; she remembered angry voices and screams of terror. She remembered everything a lifetime had tried to erase.

Her father's revelations told her enough to make her feel untethered to reality. Was her whole life a lie? She sobbed, barely holding it together until Lauren walked through the hotel room door.

Lauren arrived at the hotel shortly after five o'clock, stopping at the front desk to dial Tower's room. No answer. The clerk asked if she wanted to leave a message for him to contact her. She shook her head, deciding it would be best to confront Tower and ask him who he was and what business he *really* had in Santa Vista. Liars were easy for Lauren to spot; deceit is not a game for amateurs.

Hot, discouraged, and tired, Lauren unlocked her door, hoping a hot bath and dinner would refresh her. She was caught unaware as Marissa rushed her, threw her arms around her waist, and buried her face into Lauren's neck. She sobbed and said something unintelligible.

Tower, Lauren thought, *what has he done to hurt her?*

"Take a deep breath, count to ten, breathe again, and start over," Lauren instructed. The two moved to the side of the bed and sat, still clinging to one another. Marissa began to breathe at a steady pace. She bowed her head and confessed her fear of losing touch with reality. She was sure she was crazy.

Marissa had returned from the long beach walk with Tower and decided to nap, only to be awakened by an ominous dream. It had been like this for the past couple of nights. It felt like she was falling into a bottomless pit, only to wake with a jolt. The dreams dissolved, and only vague details remained. She could recall pieces and pictures that seemed oddly familiar. The nightmares blurred, gone but not forgotten.

"There's something I need to tell you," she whispered. "Something so wicked, so evil..." Her slender body dissolved into fits of sobs peppered with moans.

"Whatever it is, we can fix it," Lauren assured her, thinking that Tower was to blame for all this misery.

"Can you fix the fact that I'm the daughter of a murderer?" she said, raising her voice. "Makes me half evil too. What kind of life can I have carrying this secret? If I ever really loved a man, what kind of person would I be to saddle him with the daughter of a murderer? Maybe his evil gene passed on to me, or maybe I will pass it to my child. No, you must promise never to tell anyone. Promise, Lauren, look into my eyes and promise."

Marissa held her breath while she waited for Lauren's verbal oath, something she could carry to the bank. Lauren's word was gold, always.

"I promise," Lauren said. "It's your secret to share or not share."

Joan Taylor's greatest fear had reared its ugly head. She had been emphatic about her daughter not learning about her mother's murder at the hands of her father. She had been right to think that knowing about the abuse Marissa had witnessed would stir up a life best forgotten.

It was happening, but Joan didn't know. She wasn't there to help her daughter through the terror. Ben had kept his wife in the dark and decided to do what he thought was best. Joan would call it a betrayal when she learned.

Joan thought she had no reason to worry, Earl Watson could no longer harm her daughter. He was in prison and would draw his last breath there.

Chapter 32

*P*romises kept are sometimes detrimental to the person swearing you to secrecy. This would be one of those times. Marissa had made Lauren swear she wouldn't tell her mother what she was about to reveal. Lauren promised.

A few days earlier, Lauren promised Ben Taylor she would take her sister to Santa Vista for a week or so. Clearly, the young attorney was in distress following their father-daughter talk. As requested, no questions were asked. Lauren promised without reservation, knowing her father had his reasons.

All those verbal contracts had led to her current predicament; she was on her own to figure how to help her sister.

A cascade of tears and groans poured nonstop to well past midnight. Marissa's sadness gave way to panic, then returned to vulnerability. No anger, but a mixture of self-doubt and self-hate caused her to dissolve into a cascade of tears. Marissa sobbed until dawn pushed the darkness from the sky. Lauren never left her side.

Lauren's brain felt like it was going to explode. She was glad to finally hear her sister's sobs slow to a gentle snore. She pulled away, placed Marissa's head on a pillow, and covered her with a blanket. Lauren slipped into the bathroom, softly closed the door, then splashed cold water on her face. She wanted a hot shower but knew the noise would wake Marissa.

More than a shower, Lauren wanted to be alone with her thoughts. She needed time to sort out the confusion and come up with a logical plan. When she glanced into the mirror, Lauren was startled by the fearful face staring back. She knew she was in over her head.

Lauren couldn't call their mom—she had promised Marissa. She decided not to call her father. Again, she wasn't supposed to know what was going on, or at least her father wasn't ready for her to know. Ordinarily, when she got herself this deep into a dilemma, Lauren turned to Marissa and the two of them talked it out. There was always a solution.

Before yesterday, she might have approached Tower Stadler, but he was a problem unto himself. Lauren had never felt so alone, not since the night her parents were killed and the only one to comfort her was a nanny she didn't even like. Hours before, she was blowing out birthday candles and yelling at her parents. She never cried. The thought was too scary, even as a child.

This night, Lauren found herself reflecting on the time she learned of her beloved aunt's death from a heart attack. Her reaction of disbelief was as vivid as the day it happened, so many years ago. Lauren never really got over the loss; she never acknowledged her grief and made peace. She pushed the overwhelming sadness deep inside her and moved on with her life.

Lauren remembered happy times and laughed, but she never remembered loss and cried. What if she gave in to her tears and the sobs never ended? Better not to go down that road, she reasoned. Getting angry and throwing things served her best.

When rage didn't seem appropriate, Lauren turned to conversations with Aunt Sarah. She pretended the two were still only a phone call away. "You've got to help me figure this out," she whispered, lifting her eyes. "I think Marissa is in trouble and needs her mom. I can't betray a promise, but I can't stand by and do nothing."

She cracked opened the bathroom window, and a cool breeze swept over her face. She didn't have an answer, but instantly knew how to find one. "Thanks, Aunt Sarah," she said out loud.

Lauren needed to run and keep running until exhaustion forced her to concentrate solely on her breathing. Jogging with a strong wind pushing against her body always made her too tired to think. Once she quit forcing an issue, possibilities popped up out of nowhere. They didn't always make sense, but this was her way of figuring a solution for most every muddle.

She could hear her late aunt's admonishment. "The problem is, you over-think everything. Learn to trust your feelings, trust and triumph." To which, silently, Lauren punctuated her aunt's philosophy with a plea for help.

She dressed quietly, using the dawn light to find her way without knocking into furniture. She unlatched the door and heard a slight noise. The quieter she moved, the more insistent the growl. She cleared the door, pulled it shut, then laughed for the first time since yesterday. Her stomach was running low on fuel.

Lauren had skipped meals the day before, giving her full time and attention to playing detective. She stopped at the vending machine in the lobby, inserted coins, and pulled levers for cookies and crackers. She also paid for a can of cola. Carbs and caffeine, she reasoned, the breakfast of champs.

Lauren found her car and headed for the beach. First, she would jog a couple of miles. Then she would sign the lease for the vacant furnished cottage and fork over the extra $100 a month. One thing was clear: she needed to get Marissa out of the hotel. She prayed the cottage was still available. Not for Tower, though. That was another story without an ending.

Halfway through her jog, Lauren passed a taco stand and found herself ordering a breakfast burrito and coffee. She sat, picking at the food, when a man scooted next to her.

"We need to talk," he said. She turned to stare at the intruder and saw the determined face of Tower Stadler.

"*You* need to talk," she told him, "and this better be good."

He nodded. He hadn't decided on a story to explain his appearance at Price Logan's office. Tower figured he would feel her out and then come up with a plausible explanation to satisfy her curiosity.

But this was a woman who would only be satisfied with the truth; and he was obligated to protect his secret, even if it meant telling a lie. She was a reporter, after all. If details of his activities were to get out, a lawsuit would be the least of his problems.

He looked straight into her eyes and lied.

Chapter 33

Price Logan was tired, angry, and desperate. It was Monday morning, past time to be at his desk making calls and signing contracts for a planned shopping mall on the northern outskirts of Santa Vista. He had a nice chunk of cash invested in the project, which included several medium- and high-end housing communities. Half the profits would be reinvested in Logan, Inc., with the remainder parked in his private offshore accounts.

But personal problems trumped profit; Price was busy cleaning up the past. He had spent the weekend poring through the nooks and crannies of Harry Finnerty's material life, combing over each item in search of negatives he had killed to find and destroy. Price went over the clothing and furniture several times. Nothing. He felt defeated, and lack of sleep and hunger made it impossible for him to think clearly.

Price pulled a can of salted nuts and a bottle of Johnnie Walker Black from his satchel. He spread his coat on the floor, sat, and poured a single malt whisky into a coffee mug. A glance at the hands on his watch reflected the morning light. He toasted the daylight with a nightcap. Cheers.

Price gobbled handfuls of nuts and sipped at his glass. His mind was revisiting the pitiful piles of Harry's life, while his right hand reached for the bottle for several refills. It wasn't until he stood up that he felt a rush from the smooth, dark liquid. His eyes circled the warehouse, and his feet remained momentarily planted on the cement floor. His body swayed; his feet shifted to regain balance. Too little, too late; his ass hit the floor. He heard himself laughing, both observing and congratulating himself that not one drop of precious whisky had spilled.

His amusement told him he was in no shape to leave the warehouse. That and the fact that his sore ass was flat on the floor and not moving. Price rolled over and rested his head on the cool concrete floor. He decided to call his secretary to tell her he was in meetings all day. Then he would nap until late afternoon. He planned to return to the office after his secretary's car exited the garage.

Price wasn't in the mood to explain himself to anyone, least of all his secretary of 20 years. She probably knew him better than he knew himself; she could read his moods seconds after he walked in the office. The one thing he knew for sure, he wanted to be left alone to plan his next move. Damn Harry Finnerty. Damn, damn, damn him to hell.

Why did everything in his life have to be so difficult! He had lied on his university application, then nearly killed himself to make the varsity football team his sophomore year. He was living the life he dreamed, a sports hero who was admired and befriended by other popular students. He was congratulating himself on a deceit well executed on a Friday; by Saturday he was sure he'd thrown it all away in a careless moment of hormones gone wild.

All because of that bitch who wanted to score with a football player and changed her mind at the last minute. Too bad. She said she wanted him. Price had invited the star quarterback along to prove he was bedding a lovely young virgin. She wasn't going to make him a liar; he wanted a reputation as a hunk who called the shots. That's how the story went, the one he planned and played in his daydreams.

He didn't want to be the son of a coal miner. He didn't want to be poor. He didn't want to be Frankie Fletcher. Formal schooling ended his junior year in high school when his father signed him up to work in the coal mines. But the young teen had other ideas.

He ran away from home at age 16, picked up odd jobs for a year, then enrolled at the university as Price Logan. The first few years he earned money hawking course papers for his teammates. Logic and rhetoric came easily, always had since he began to read and write at age five.

Handsome and clever, he was sure he was born for better things, and off he went to find his fame and fortune.

Fame came his sophomore year when his name appeared on the varsity football roster. Fortune came a few years later when the daughter of a business tycoon set her sights on becoming Mrs. Price Logan.

She was wealthy, beautiful, and told Price he had stolen her heart. Madeline McCabe made love to his ego weeks before she allowed him to make love to her body. Shrewd and calculating, she was tying her future to a man she knew would soar to greater heights than her father. She lusted for power and position of her own.

Her passionate lovemaking was new to him; he felt parts of his body come alive and scream for more. Their bodies entwined, and she brought him to a new awareness of his own sexuality. He wanted more pleasure. She wanted to get pregnant.

They both got their way when Price and Madeline faced the preacher, promising love, loyalty, "and lust," she whispered in his ear. His graduate school diploma read "MBA." Madeline's read "MRS."

She made love to him that night, teaching his body new heights of passion. When they woke the next morning, Madeline turned to her new husband and asked if he had enjoyed their lovemaking.

"Oh, baby," he said, reaching for her plump breasts.

"Remember it, because that's the last time you will ever touch me," she said, matter-of-fact. When they arrived home later that day, she retired to her bedroom, bolted the lock, and kept her word. He would never be allowed to see, touch, or hold her naked body "till death do they part."

Seven months later, a daughter was born but never lived to celebrate her first birthday. Doctors consoled Madeline, assuring her these things happen and that there would be other children. No one consoled Price; he knew there would never be more children to love. He closed his heart and bolted it shut. Price turned his time and talent into growing companies instead of a family. His companies spawned new companies and he nurtured them as lovingly as if they were his children.

Madeline became reclusive and eventually died alone in her bed of a drug overdose. He buried her on a cold December morning, packed his clothes, and drove west. Price never endured another frozen winter, but his heart never thawed.

Price woke from his nap in the late afternoon and headed from the warehouse to the coffee shop across the street from his office to sit and wait for his secretary to leave. He sipped coffee and rubbed his temples. It was going to be a long rest of the day.

He wasn't drunk, but he wasn't sober either. Price Logan was staring at his office building when he first saw the impossible. "Please God, no," he whispered. His mind flashed back to a snowy forest clearing in 1941. Price was watching a ghost from the past walk into his building. He rushed across the street to see where the man was going and watched as he stepped into the express elevator to his company headquarters.

The man turned around, smiled. Price clutched at his stomach, turned, and ran. He needed to find a lonely stretch of beach and inhale salty air until his brain cleared. The world was closing in on him; he needed to think.

Perhaps the time had come to escape to the Cayman Islands, collect his millions, then disappear. It would cost him millions that he would need to leave behind, along with his reputation, but what good is a reputation to a madman? Had the past reared its ugly head and come back to demand justice? *How do you know if you're going crazy? How long does it take?*

"Please God, no," he said, turning his car west to find warm sand to thwart the icy chill crawling up and down his spine.

Chapter 34

*E*arly morning runs along the waterfront in Seattle were Tower Stadler's wake-up ritual and had been since his freshman year when he joined the high school track team. It continued through college and became as addictive as a chunk of cheddar on a slice of warm apple pie.

This day, the California coastal mist that coated and cooled his body suited him; it eased him into the day like an oldie tune from the radio. Seattle rain was more like a fire truck siren, loud and obnoxious.

Tower thought how easy it would be to get used to this place and its people, especially the young reporter he met on the plane a couple of days ago. Lauren Foster, he remembered, then laughed when he saw her 50 feet down the boardwalk. She was sitting on a bench munching on a burrito.

Tower knew he needed to stop and talk if he had any chance of soliciting her silence. As he approached, he slowed his pace from a jog to a casual trot, mentally rehearsing a conversation to justify his recent actions. He filled his lungs with salt air, then slowly exhaled and shook his hands to loosen his apprehension.

Tower was good at lying, both personally and professionally, so he felt the yarn he was about to spin would placate Lauren.

"We need to talk," he said. When she turned and looked him straight in the eyes, he felt a momentary pause. Suddenly, he wasn't so sure about how to handle the situation. He realized he liked her more than he thought, maybe too much. This feeling was new to him and wasn't going to get him across the finish line. He dismissed his emotions and turned his attention to the job at hand. He didn't even blink.

Lauren wanted an explanation about his emergence from Price's private office as a telephone repairman. She finished his sentence with an ominous warning: "And it had better be good."

He was a seasoned liar, but he was beginning to think her "liar radar" would detect his lack of veracity. Then what? Truth was out of the question. He trusted no one. And, besides, this truth wasn't his to tell. The fact that she was a newspaper reporter made the situation black and white. He had to lie as if his current assignment depended on it. Because it did.

"First, I'm asking you to promise me that this conversation, at least the first part, is off the record," he said. "I sense that your journalistic integrity is a big part of who you are as a person. I'm counting on that." He waited for a confirmation.

Lauren countered: "I'm not big on blind faith. Part of me wants to trust you and part of me thinks there's something very wrong about you. It's a puzzle, and I'm usually on target with first impressions. But, honestly, I can't get a read on you."

"Go with your first impression, at least till you hear me out," he said.

She nodded.

"Okay, here goes. I'm not here looking for work. I've got a job. In fact, I own a thriving design and construction firm," he continued. "I put our financial future on the line. I invested a year's worth of my time and hundreds of thousands of dollars to get the contract on the new shopping center north of the city. The Santa Vista town council loved our design, and our bid was the lowest.

"Then, last week, I got word that the contract was awarded to Price Industries. I saw the designs, looked over their budget, and there's no legitimate way the project should have been awarded to Price."

"You suspect a payoff?" Lauren interrupted.

Tower's breathing slowed; she was following his lead.

"That's what I want to find out," he said. "A friend at the phone company put static on the lines so there would be a repair order. I wanted to look around Price's office." He stopped talking, put his hand over Lauren's, and thanked her for pretending not to know him yesterday when he came bounding out of the office.

"I found something to make me think I'm on the right track, but if a newspaper reporter starts nosing around, a certain councilman will make sure there's no evidence to prove what I'm thinking."

"Okay, so what do you want from me, other than keeping my nose out of it?"

Tower looked at Lauren and proposed a deal to share information once he had it nailed. "Marissa filled me in on some details about the old guy who was run over and killed after leaving Price's office," Tower said. "Is it possible that the reporter found out about some illegal dealings? Do you think Harry was there to confront Price or, worse, was Harry there to demand hush money not to print what he knew?"

Tower zoomed in on something else Marissa had told him. Another recent unexplained death, homicide really, for such a small community. He followed that train of thought: "Like Harry's death. And then cops found a second unidentified body at the donation store. Can the two deaths be linked?"

He was putting words to her thoughts. Something was going on and it appealed to her professional curiosity. Lauren was scheduled to report back to work the next day, so why not follow a couple of leads bouncing around her brain?

"And, once you piece this together, I get the exclusive?" Lauren asked. He agreed.

The two shook hands on the deal and went their separate ways. He felt bad that she was headed for a series of dead ends, but the next few days would give him time to wrap up his assignment and get out of town. His would be a hollow victory. Another chance at love lost.

Chapter 35

*L*auren rented the furnished cottage for a week, agreeing to pay extra until she could outfit Harry's old cottage and move back. She asked Tower to collect Marissa and their belongings the next morning while she was at work. He drove her to the newspaper at nine on Wednesday, then kept the car for the day.

Everything was working out well. The kids at the beach begged to have Charlee Bear for a sleepover and it seemed like the perfect solution since Lauren couldn't bring the dog to the hotel. Betty had been good about giving Charlee room and board, and she agreed to let the kids have a turn.

After getting the okay from their mom, the kids showed up at Betty's door to collect Charlee. Elia snapped the leash on Charlee's collar, not that he needed any reason to stay close to the young girl. Charlee adored Elia. Betty handed Benj the dog's dinner in a paper sack and reminded him to take along Charlee's bed. Benj took the food, thanked Betty, and grabbed a corner of Charlee's overstuffed bed from under the lemon tree. He hurried to his sister's side, dragging the bed behind him.

"We're here," Elia squealed. Her mom opened the kitchen door and watched as a parade of dog and kids bounded inside. She let out a yelp when she spotted the wet, sandy dog bed leave a brown trail on her newly mopped floor.

"Whoa," she told Benj. "That filthy dog bed needs a good washing." Benj dropped his grip on the bed, then scampered off to wrestle with Charlee and their puppy, Rose.

Their mom sniffed the lumpy bed and walked outside to give it a good shake. Clearly, Benj had dragged it through puddles and sand. She unzipped the cover, shook it again, and headed for the washing machine, where she tossed it in with several beach towels, turned the setting to hot water, and added an extra squirt of detergent.

She decided to let the guts of Charlee's bed air out and slung it over a chair. That's when she noticed stuffing oozing out of one corner. A needle and thread would fix the problem.

She placed the bed on the patio table and flattened the stuffing with her hands, pulling back when a sharp edge glanced her right palm. She pulled at the lumps and spotted the culprit—camera negatives in a frosted cellophane sleeve. She placed the object on the kitchen counter, planning to put the film in an envelope so the kids could return it to Lauren when they brought Charlee home Wednesday morning.

Chapter 36

Back in Seattle, Joan returned home from her Monday night hospital shift. Only five o'clock and it was already dark. She picked at some leftovers from the refrigerator and then headed to bed. The weekend festivities had left her happy but exhausted, and she was a bit relieved that she had the evening to herself since Ben was on a quick business trip.

Joan woke up refreshed early Tuesday to the smell of freshly brewed coffee. She joined Evelyn, and the two women sat sipping coffee and swapping news.

Evelyn told her how much she had enjoyed the party and thanked her again for including her in the festivities. "You both have been like family to me," she said. "I am so proud of the kids and how well life is turning out for all of you."

Joan went to collect the mail on Ben's desk when she spotted a white envelope with "Ben" scribbled on the front. She called out to Evelyn to ask her about it.

"Oh, that," Evelyn said. "An old fraternity brother showed up at the door, said he hadn't seen Ben for years and wanted to surprise him. I told him he was on a business trip till Wednesday, and he seemed awfully disappointed. Wrote Ben that note and left."

Funny, Joan didn't remember her husband joining a fraternity, didn't seem like the type then or now. Parties bored him. He didn't like beer and wasn't particularly fond of sports. Maybe it was a business fraternity, she thought, then made a mental note to ask him.

The phone rang just as she was leaving for the hospital. It was Ben. He called to hear her voice and tell her how much she was loved. Joan never tired of hearing those precious three words, "I love you."

"By the way," she said, "an old fraternity brother dropped by yesterday to surprise you. Evelyn told him you were away on a business trip, so he left you a note. I didn't know you were in a fraternity. Which one?"

"There's a lot you still don't know about me," Ben laughed, "and I intend to remain somewhat of a mystery to keep you captivated. Gotta run, Joan. Love you."

She heard the click on the other end of the line, stared at the receiver, shrugged and left for work. Ben gave her ten minutes to collect her purse and keys and leave for work before redialing his home. Ben wanted to speak to Evelyn, alone.

"Taylor residence," Evelyn answered.

"Evelyn, it's Ben. I wanted to ask about the note, but Joan had to rush off to work. I'm curious which of my fraternity brothers bothered to drop by after so many years. Open the note and read it to me, would you please?"

Evelyn put the phone down, returned to his office, and brought the note to the foyer. She opened the envelope, stared at the blank piece of paper, and left to check for another envelope. Nothing.

"Odd thing, Mr. Taylor, I opened the envelope but there's no writing, just a blank piece of writing paper folded to fit in the envelope. I checked to see if there was another note, but only the regular bills came in the mail yesterday. Bills and this envelope, nothing else on the desk addressed to you."

"Evelyn, think back and describe this man to me. How old was he? How tall? What else did he say?"

"Something wrong, Mr. Taylor? Shouldn't I have let him in? I was in your office most of the time he was there. Just came to finish dusting the living room when he handed me the note and left. He couldn't have been alone for more than a couple minutes. Did I do something wrong?"

"Take a deep breath and tell me about the visit, from the time you opened the door until the time he left," Ben said. "Anything peculiar, any questions?"

She went over the visit, from the moment she met him until the time he left.

"Now I remember, said his name was Jules, didn't catch the last name, if he gave it to me." She told Ben about his throat spasm when he was sitting at the desk. Told him about the interest in the girls. Told him she talked about them and how Lauren had gotten a job at the newspaper in Santa Vista. Told him the girls were there, left earlier yesterday morning on a plane for Santa Vista."

He told Evelyn to reseal the note and not to say anything more about the incident to Joan. "Nothing."

That same Tuesday, the man who had left the note for Ben was driving into the town of Santa Vista. More tired than angry, he stopped for his usual hamburger, cola, and fries, then found a motel on the cheaper south side of the city. He needed sleep and a shower before he started the search for his daughter.

Chapter 37

Tower dropped Lauren off at the newspaper shortly before nine, then headed back to the hotel to pick up Marissa and move her into the cottage. He planned to spend at least half the day relaxing on the beach after checking in with the San Francisco office to give them the heads-up on the Price Logan situation.

Swift and successful, per usual.

He would devote the afternoon to composing his letter of resignation from the FBI. Tower wanted it to be short and to the point; the Bureau had misused a valuable agent and was losing him as a result. He desperately wanted management to acknowledge how badly they had treated him, and, more importantly, he wanted to know why he hadn't been named to head the major crimes division.

Tower pulled the car into an empty space at the front of the hotel and honked; Marissa had promised to be packed and waiting in the lobby. She came bounding out a minute later, trailed by a pushcart loaded with several suitcases. Tower got out from behind the driver's seat and opened the passenger door.

He hit the lever to push the seat forward and load the backseat with their belongings. Once done, he pushed the seat as far back as it would go before it locked into place.

Marissa settled into the seat and reached down to retrieve an envelope on the floor before securing her seat belt.

"Dropped this," she said, handing him the envelope. He turned and placed it on top of his briefcase.

"And while I'm giving you things," she said, "I found this picture tucked in the pocket of Lauren's khaki jacket. Who's the guy with you, and why the funny clothes?"

Tower took the picture from her, scanned the black-and-white images, and shrugged. His poker face hid equal parts confusion and anger. It wasn't him in the picture yet there he was. He stuck the photo in his jacket pocket and changed the subject. "Let's get you out of this place and into the warm sunshine."

The two chatted on the drive. Thoughtless but polite conversation filled the car. Both were lost in a world of questions with no answers on the horizon, at least none acceptable. When the car pulled up, Charlee Bear met them curbside with so much enthusiasm he nearly knocked Marissa to the ground. She giggled, and Tower heard himself laughing out loud.

He pulled the key from his pocket, along with the mystery photo Marissa handed to him outside the hotel. He tossed the photo on the driver's seat and unloaded the suitcases from the car, taking them to the cottage door. He hurried back to park the car.

Tower icked up the snapshot again, glancing at the two men as he turned the car wheels left then right, stopping when the VW was centered between white lines. He put the car in park, switched off the engine, and continued to stare at the photo. The man on the left was his father. His face drained of all color. The second man in the photo was a much younger version of Price Logan. What the hell?

He placed the two photos side-by-side. Tower squinted to examine the photos for details. The first, the photo Marissa found in Lauren's jacket pocket, showed two college buddies laughing at a football game. In the second, the same two men but this time panic was written all over their faces. They were bent over the lifeless body of a young woman.

He needed answers and decided to go looking for Price Logan.

When he grabbed his briefcase, the envelope on top slid onto his lap. Tower noticed the return address, Harry Finnerty's beach address. He unsealed the envelope and pulled the contents out. He found a black-and-white photograph sandwiched between the folds of a letter.

The man on the left holding a woman's limp head was his father; the other man was Price Logan. A stamp on the back read: "Photography by Harry Finnerty."

The letter was addressed to the parents of Tina Stewart, Chicago, Illinois: "If you are reading this letter it's because I am dead, murdered probably. I had occasion to take this picture in December of 1941. I was secretly tailing two varsity football players, Tom Stadler and Price Logan, for a feature story to run in the university's newspaper, figured on 'a day in the life of' these popular guys. I never came forward because I feared for my life. I am sorry I could not be brave but there you have it. I always thought you deserved to know the truth about what happened to your daughter." It was signed, "Harry Finnerty."

Chapter 38

Tower Stadler's brain was scrambling to make sense of it all. Both photographs were seared into his eyeballs, but he couldn't process details to digest and file the new information. Moments and memories moved as fast as a race horse galloping to the finish line. He felt like a mute passenger in a foreign country, gazing out the window. He couldn't read the signs. Too much, too fast. Everything was a blur.

This new territory totally discombobulated the FBI agent who thought he'd seen and heard it all.

Tower heard a rap on the car window and turned to see Marissa. She was frowning, something was wrong. With her? he thought. Tower saw her finger pointing to the steering wheel; he saw what she saw. His fingers were ashen. The veins on the back of his hands bulged and pulsated. When he let go, a violent pain raced up and down his arms.

"What happened, you all right?" Marissa said. "You don't look well."

"Heartburn," he lied. Then he wasn't so sure. His heart hurt, another new feeling. Was his father really a murderer? Was this the something so bad that it made the present intolerable and any future hopeless?

Tower had always thought his father's pain stemmed from the horrors of war, man's inhumanity inflicted on his enemy. For that he could be forgiven. But this?

He wanted to turn to Marissa and blurt out the words, "I just found out my father was a murderer." But how could anyone understand the searing pain, the sense of betrayal in that one sentence. He felt branded as the son of a murderer, a man condemned to pay for the sins of his father. He felt damaged by proxy.

Tower opened the car door and told Marissa he needed to go for a jog to release his excess energy. She offered to change clothes and come with him but stopped mid-sentence. He clearly wanted to be alone with his thoughts.

Marissa was planning to head back to the cottage to unpack when she heard her stomach object. She had skipped breakfast and the cupboards were bare in Lauren's new cottage. She told Tower she was going to the market and asked if he wanted her to pick up anything.

"Beer," he grunted, then raced down the boardwalk. Tears escaped his eyes; he told himself it was out of anger, but even he knew better. Tower's sorrow was for his father.

His was a life not lived decades before his body was lowered into the ground.

Too occupied to notice, Tower didn't see the man in the shadows of a nearby palm tree.

Price Logan, the other man in both photos, sat with his body resting on the hood of a light green sedan. He was watching the cottage, waiting for Lauren, and hoping her movements would lead him to the pictures he was sure she had.

Maybe Harry had told her about the photos before he died, since she was with him when it happened. Maybe she found them before he was able to empty the apartment. Otherwise, why was she poking around?

But speculating wasn't good enough; Price needed answers. He was on a search-and-destroy mission and vowed to bring it to a satisfactory conclusion, no matter the damage.

Indecision froze Price the second he saw Tower move down the boardwalk. Follow a ghost from the past or wait for Lauren Foster? He stayed put. He was rewarded when a taxi deposited the object of his obsession: Lauren Foster. She bolted from cab to cottage, grabbed the car keys, and zoomed down the main street heading for downtown. Price was about to follow when he saw his ghost jogging in his direction.

Their eyes connected. A confrontation was inevitable.

Chapter 39

*E*arl Watson parked his rental car across the street from the newspaper's main entrance. A huge truck gave him the cover he needed to see and not be seen. He had stopped at the market for sandwiches and soda, lunch and dinner in case he needed to be there all day. But the wait wasn't long.

Lauren Foster, dressed in black slacks, white shirt, and red blazer, emerged from the office building and hailed a cab. She looked just like the picture he had seen on Ben's desk.

He turned over the engine and felt his heart race. Soon, he told himself. Soon, he would be able to make things right with his daughter. Patience, he promised himself. He never dreamed this day would come and he was having trouble wrapping his mind around the possibilities. He realized he was talking out loud and scanned his surroundings to make sure no one was staring. Only crazy people talk to themselves, everybody knew that.

The Yellow Cab pulled up by some cottages on the beach. Earl pulled his car into a nearby parking lot. He heard raised voices just yards away. Two men were arguing. Lauren saw the men and called out a name. One looked up and waved, the other took off running.

Earl slumped in his seat and put his hand over his eyes for shade. He had meant to pick up sunglasses or a hat at the corner market but got distracted. He made a mental note to get them on his way back to the motel.

Earl couldn't hear what Lauren and the handsome stranger were saying, but he got the impression that he liked her a whole lot more than she liked him. Earl was picking apart their body language when a third person emerged from the shadows and joined them.

She took his breath away. Marie. Sweet Marie. His Marie.

Earl was content to just watch his daughter; he hadn't planned what he would say to her, never got that far. She looked a lot like her mother, but Marie had her father's hair and slim build. He wondered what her voice would sound like but didn't dare move any closer. Later, he told himself, there would be plenty of time later.

Lauren left to go inside one of the cottages, then came back and got into her VW, parked not far from his car. Earl knew she saw him; she was the type to be aware of most everything and everyone around her. Cautious, yes, but not fearful. She seemed very sure of herself and Earl was suddenly glad that Lauren was such a good friend to Marie. Was his daughter like that? Was she bold or shy? Did she go after what she wanted or just take what came her way?

For now, Earl Watson was just grateful to see Marie's face. He nixed any plans to approach her. He decided to grab the soda on the passenger seat and go sit on the sand to enjoy the sound of the waves. Of course, that would mean walking right by Marie. And that would be okay. If she looked up, he might even say a casual hello.

But Marissa and Tower had moved on by the time he got out of the car. That was okay, he told himself. There was so much new information to entertain him. He had been sitting for hours when he heard a voice speaking to him.

"Huh," he said, realizing he had dozed off.

"Your face is all red, and you have an awful sunburn," the woman said. "Get some aloe vera gel and put it on your face when you get home, and stay out of the sun for a few days. Next time you should wear a hat."

The woman walked past him, then clapped at the sight of a big red dog and a small blonde puppy galloping toward her. Two small children tried unsuccessfully to keep pace with the dogs. They collapsed on the sand once they reached Marissa.

Elia reached in her back pocket and offered an envelope to Marissa. "Mommy said to give you these negatives. She found them in Charlee Bear's bed when she took it apart to wash it. We kind of got it wet and sandy dragging it to our house. Sorry."

Marissa stuffed the envelope in a back pocket and ran off to catch Charlee playing in the waves. Rose followed and chased Elia. Benj caught up with them and muttered, "Those dogs can sure wear me out."

Earl watched and listened. Kids and dogs were a good judge of character and it sure seemed both liked his daughter a lot. He smiled, remembering the first words his daughter had said to him. "Your face is all red." If he died this moment, he was sure he had been given the gift of a glimpse into heaven.

A man with binoculars watched the exchange and felt a sense of relief. He knew where the film was; now all he had to do was get it away from the blonde wearing the purple T-shirt and blue jeans.

Marissa was oblivious to anything except the kids and dogs. Tired from unpacking and grocery shopping, she was glad to get out into the sun and wiggle her toes in the sand. And the wonderful greetings from Charlee and the kids made the sunshine seem even warmer.

She had tried to get Tower to spend the rest of the morning with her, but he said he needed to make some phone calls and would be back after lunch. It was now after one o'clock, and she realized he wasn't coming.

Tower had spent the time trying to figure out his next move. He had told Stevens the job was done. But would he tell the Bureau about these photos? For years, the FBI had been trying to get evidence of white-collar crimes committed by Price Logan. Tower had it within his power to hand the Bureau Logan's head on a platter. Murder One. But the very proof that condemned Price Logan also would ruin the name of his dead father, Tom Stadler.

Tower's one and only conversation with Price sealed the older man's fate. Price was arrogant and corrupt, and he would do anything necessary to get what he wanted.

Tower wouldn't tell Price about the photos; the jerk would find out when Agent Bill Stevens put the cuffs on him. He called the San Francisco office, dialing the private number for this assignment. Tower told Bill Stevens everything, photo proof and all.

He told him about the millions held in offshore banks in the Cayman Islands, gave him the names of the banks along with a second name attached to these accounts: Walt Langdon.

"Don't know if he's a partner or a pseudonym for Price," Tower said. "Get a pen and I'll give you the numbers. Freeze the funds. This guy is ready to bolt."

When Lauren returned to work, she received an urgent telegram. She called the telegraph office to collect the message and a voice on the other end began reading: "Life or death *stop* Meet me at Santa Vista bus terminal 1 p.m. *stop* Come alone *stop* Don't tell Marissa." It was signed, "Dad."

Lauren felt confused and worried. What could be going on that was a matter of life and death? Was there more her sister wasn't telling her? The more Marissa kept things churning inside, the bigger they became until problems were catastrophic. Had Marissa reached out in panic to her father?

She hung up the telephone and raced to the bus station. She pulled in the terminal lot seconds after his bus arrived. Ben's face was as gray as the trail of smoke spewing from the bus's exhaust pipes.

"Thank God, Lauren," Ben said, loading an overnight case in her backseat. "I've put myself out on a limb and it seems the weight is about to send me crashing to the pavement. Don't ask me why I did any of what I am about to tell you because there is no rhyme or reason. It's done, and now I have to figure a way to minimize the damage about to be done to Marissa and my wife."

He proceeded to tell her everything he had confessed to Marissa during their conversation in the garden. The hardest part was telling Lauren about betraying his wife. She would be more hurt than angry when she found out her husband had gone behind her back. He still held out hope that she would never need to be told.

Then he told her something not even Marissa knew. Her biological father had learned the whereabouts of his daughter, Marie. Ben explained that Earl Watson had come to the house under false flags and learned information from their housekeeper that would direct him straight to Santa Vista.

"He may already be here, probably is here," Ben said. "I don't know the man or what his intentions are toward Marissa. He went to jail because of his uncontrollable anger and I don't know that much of that can be tamed in a prison environment."

He told Lauren he was frightened for his daughter; and his face reflected panic.

Chapter 40

*E*arl Watson's hands and feet were beet red, and if the burn on his face looked as bad as it felt, the night ahead was going to be painful. He stood up, rolled down his pant legs, then shook the sand from his shoes and socks.

He headed up the beach, crossed the sidewalk, and headed toward his rental car. Earl opened the windows to let the car cool and took a bite of his roast beef sandwich. He was mesmerized; his daughter was laughing as she played tag with kids and dogs. He had missed so much time with her, but that was going to change, he promised himself.

He reached over to grab a napkin, wiped mustard off his face, then tossed the dirty lunch bag into a nearby trash can. And that's when he heard the screams. First one, then a chorus. One of the two men he had seen arguing earlier that morning had grabbed his daughter and was pulling her up the beach.

The old man yelled at the kids and kicked sand at the dogs. He was heading straight for Earl with Marissa in tow. She looked like a raggedy doll, using all her energy to reason with the man.

Earl sprinted to rescue his daughter. He tackled the man as Marissa ran back to the beach and the safety of the gathering crowd. Earl took a swing and missed; Price Logan connected and sent the ex-con reeling backward onto the concrete curb. Price grabbed the envelope he had dropped, raced to his car, and took the exit out of the lot on two wheels.

Marissa ordered the kids to run home and then darted toward the lifeless stranger on the sidewalk with his neck twisted forward in the sand. She yelled for someone to call an ambulance and knelt at his side.

She took his hand in hers, wiped tears from her eyes with her shoulder, and pleaded with the stranger to open his eyes. In a quiet voice, she promised not to leave his side until the medics got there. But he never opened his eyes. He never saw his lovely Marie again.

Lauren and Ben pulled into the beach parking lot soon after the ambulance arrived. Charlee Bear espied Lauren and came running, barking and whining, trying to make her understand that he wanted her to follow. Lauren saw Marissa and understood. Ben trailed not far behind.

"Oh, Lauren," Marissa wailed, "he's dead! Some man was after me and this stranger helped me get away. And he's dead, the other guy hit him with his fist and knocked him to the ground. It all happened so fast, I don't understand any of it. Do you suppose he thought I was you? What kind of trouble have you gotten yourself into, Lauren?"

Ben walked over to the dead man and pulled back the sheet covering his face. He looked up at Lauren, nodded, and mouthed the words, "It's Earl."

An officer told Ben the man had no identification on him, just an AA token in his pocket. Ben planned to retrieve the token and make sure it was given to Marissa from "the stranger" who had come to her rescue.

Tower walked toward the crowd and stopped near Lauren. "What happened?"

"I don't know," Lauren said. "But I'd bet any amount of money that you could tell me."

Ben joined them and introductions were made. Ben and Lauren turned to have a private conversation, ending with "It dies here." Marissa wouldn't be told that the dead man, her hero, was her biological father. Let her believe in the goodness of strangers, they agreed.

Then Tower took hold of Lauren's elbow and steered her near a man in a gray-striped suit and yellow tie. The three of them walked to a black sedan parked on the outskirts of the lot. Tower ordered Lauren to get in.

"Not until you tell me what's going on and who you really are," she said.

Tower reached in his coat pocket, took out his FBI identification, and told Lauren getting in the car wasn't a request but rather an order. "You are in protective custody until I say you're not."

Tower had been shadowing Price Logan since their earlier confrontation; he knew the man would kill to get what he wanted. If Earl Watson hadn't stepped in, Tower would have a few moments later. He saw Elia hand Marissa an envelope and noted how jumpy it made Price Logan. Probably the same negative he had seen earlier. Tower surmised that the envelope was the object of Price's interest and not Marissa. She was just one more person in his way.

Tower located a telephone and filled FBI senior Bill Stevens on the day's turn. He agreed with Tower: Lauren was to stay in his protective custody for the time.

Plans were in process to arrest Price Logan, but he bolted before his capture and confinement. Stevens did get a federal judge to flag the Cayman Island accounts. The monies would be frozen once proof was offered of Price's involvement in the murder of a young woman. No statute of limitations could save Price Logan from a murder conviction. And he knew it.

Price Logan had left the scene in a panic; he had the film but had caused such a stir, he knew the police would be after him.

He had a Plan B for the unforeseen: Flee the country, change his name, and live in luxury with the money he had stolen and stashed in offshore banks.

His first stop was an apartment he had rented under the name of Walter Langdon. He raced across town, parked his car in an alley, and removed the license plates, swapping them with another car nearby.

He packed his clothes in two suitcases, then found a large leather satchel and filled it with cash from his wall safe. It wasn't a lot, but it would serve him until he could claim his offshore millions.

Finally, he grabbed a set of car keys and two passports from a desk drawer—one read Price Logan, the second Walter Langdon.

He left the apartment, locked the door, and walked two flights down to the underground parking area. He put the luggage in the backseat of an older model sedan and headed for the freeway.

Fate had demanded his reputation, but his brilliant mind and business savvy would assure a new life and the chance to start over. Price filled the gas tank on the way out of town, then merged onto the Interstate 5 south freeway ramp.

Next stop: Mexico. He found himself singing the words with Kenny Rogers' hot tune. "Know when to hold 'em; know when to fold 'em; know when to walk away, and know when to run."

Chapter 41

Something was happening to Lauren that was neither familiar nor welcome. Two things she did know: She wanted to be alone, and she desperately needed to hide the tears threatening to pour out her eyeballs. All this upset but her stomach was calm. It was her heart that ached.

She excused herself and turned to run down the boardwalk, but not before Tower grabbed her arm and informed her that she was in his custody. Where she went, he followed.

"I'm serious about this," Tower said. "I have some information that you need to know for your own safety, nothing that you can print in the *Journal*. Later, just not now. So, I'm not letting you out of my sight."

She turned, pounded on his chest with her fists, then burst into sobs. Her body shook; he held her close. "This has been a hard day for all of us, and I envy you," Tower whispered. "I wish I could cry. God knows I have enough reason to sit down and give in to my emotions. I've never done that, not even as a child."

Lauren looked up at Tower, her face frozen. "I'm the one who never cries," she said. "But I'm scared, for the first time in my life. I think I am going to fall and die because there's nobody there to catch me."

"Talk to me, Lauren, you can trust me," he said. "What's really going on?"

"It's not my truth to tell," Lauren said, "but the lies, and now Ben wants to tell more lies. My family is in trouble and there's nothing I can do to make it stop." She swallowed the last word, and her body began to shake again.

Tower tightened his arms around Lauren and rested his chin on the top of her head. He realized he cared deeply about this woman. Maybe he even was beginning to fall in love. When did *that* happen? he wondered silently.

"Okay, let's walk near the jetty and sit on the rocks," he said. "Neither one of us is feeling steady on our feet."

Lauren nodded. As sad as she was, the feeling of being totally alone was easing. Maybe she could talk to this man who was so much like herself.

"Ben has told too many lies to come clean," she said, "and he thinks it's too late for the truth. But I think he must come clean if there's going to be any chance for this family. Marissa just learned a lot about her past, but not the whole truth. I can't talk about it without breaking confidences. But I can tell you this—if Ben doesn't hold a family meeting and take responsibility, there will be no future of love and trust. I need to speak up, but it's really not my place."

"Since when did you think not telling the truth, that lying, was okay?" Tower said. "You know better than that, and I know you know better than that. So, what aren't you telling me? Why are you feeling so defeated?"

"I wish I knew you better, enough to trust you," she said. "There's something you're hiding and it makes me not want to trust you. I can't talk this over with Marissa because Ben's the problem. Ben's supposed to be the one with all the answers, the one who always does what's right."

"A father can lie with his words; a father can lie by his silence," Tower said, looking out at the ocean waves. "I know. My world just got tossed on its head and there are some hard decisions ahead. I can't even bring myself to think about them. I wish I could go back to yesterday and unknow what I know. If that makes any sense."

"The truth is always better, right?"

"Unless it's so terrible that you can't live with it," Tower said. "But when you run away from the truth and hide, you forfeit any real happiness. You forfeit any real life."

"I know I want to confront Ben and tell him he's wrong," Lauren said. "He can tell the truth and we will all be better off. I know it. I just don't know if it's my place. What if he confesses the lies, tells the whole truth, and then Joan and Marissa won't forgive him? How can I take that responsibility?"

"I get it," he said. "More than I can tell you, at least for now. Go with your gut; the gut never lies."

Lauren turned and hugged him. She put her head on his chest and heard his heart beat fast and strong. She wanted to stay there a moment longer but decided to go find Ben while she still had the nerve.

"I need to talk to him in private," she said. "You can't be there."

"Not there, but nearby," Tower scolded. "I meant what I said—you don't go anywhere without my eyes on you."

The two walked back to the cottage to find Ben. Lauren had an urge to hold Tower's hand but thought better of it. She wanted his strength, nothing more, or so she told herself.

Tower waited outside the front door to the cottage while Lauren spoke with Ben. He heard her first few words before the door closed: "I need to tell you something you probably don't want to hear."

After ten minutes, Tower saw Marissa approach the cottage gate. He walked up to her, offering his sympathy for what she had been through. He asked her to sit outside for a moment; Lauren wanted to have a private conversation with Ben.

She heard his words, nodded, and sat. Charlee Bear came rushing up to Marissa and settled his big head on her lap. She got out of the chair, sat on the ground, and pulled Charlee onto her lap. More minutes passed before the cottage door opened. Marissa had seen a lot of strange things this day, but this was the strangest of all. Lauren was crying. Not just a little. She was bawling.

The look on Ben's face told her he, too, was very sad. Just no tears.

"We need to talk," Ben told Marissa, "and I think now is a good time. Lauren and I agreed that it should be just you and me. She'll be right outside."

Marissa turned to look at Lauren. Lauren's eyes faced the ground. "Don't be frightened. I just can't be there for you right now. You're in for a shock, but it's going to be all right. We have to get through this as a family."

Ben pulled a metal token from his pocket and told his daughter to come in and sit down.

A half hour later, the two walked out, neither smiling nor crying.

"It's a lot to digest," Marissa told Lauren. "The hardest part is that Dad has to tell this to Mom. He's flying home to talk with her tonight."

Then she changed the subject.

"Can you guys go to the morgue with me? I want to say goodbye and thanks to a man I have hated ever since I was told about him. I'll never call him Dad, but he gave me life and then gave his life to save mine.

"And I want to put this token back in his pocket," Marissa said. "It's the only way I know to say thank you."